Chris Wooding

SCHOLASTIC
PRESS

Look out for other books
by Chris Wooding:

_ *Kerosene: Catchman*

Scholastic Children's Books,
Commonwealth House, 1–19 New Oxford Street,
London WC1A 1NU, UK
a division of Scholastic Ltd
London ~ New York ~ Toronto ~ Sydney ~ Auckland

First published in the UK by Scholastic Ltd, 1998

Lyrics taken from *Surrendering the Ghost* are reproduced
by kind permission of Chamberlain.

ISBN 0 590 54347 4

Typeset by DP Photosetting, Aylesbury, Bucks.
Printed by Cox and Wyman Ltd, Reading, Berks.

10 9 8 7 6 5 4 3 2 1

To Tricia Henderson and Terry Everley,
who had more faith in me than I did.

"I remember keeping mad hours in the night
Beneath an honest sky
When a world of shadows stood at shoulder side by side
And so did you and I"

Chamberlain, *Surrendering the Ghost*

Chapter One

I still couldn't get over how nice a day it was, even at seven o'clock in the evening (or roundabout that time) when Danny Forester turned up at my house.

The street that I live on is set into quite a steep hill, y'see. My house – number 105 – is somewhere near the middle. In the summertime, towards the tail-end of the day, you can see the sun dipping beneath the rooftops of the houses at the top of the hill. The light comes shining straight along the road like a laser beam, carved up by the long shadows of the chimney stacks. And on this particular day, when the air was just the right temperature and there was just the faintest hint of a breeze, it looked pretty damn wonderful, I can tell you.

Anyway, I'd wandered out of my front door on that summer's day, having made the house as ready as I possibly could for the party, and there was Danny, ambling down the hill, with the sunlight outlining him in dazzling gold. He was like that; he just seemed to have a certain natural *style* about him. If it had been anyone else, they'd have probably come up the hill the other way, squinting into the sun and shading their eyes as they came. But Danny, though; if I hadn't known better, I'd say he made a detour just so

1

he could be walking with the sun at his back. He looked like the Second Coming or something.

I sat down on the edge of the garden wall and sparked up a tab while I was waiting for him to get here. I don't normally smoke – I worry too much about all the crap that goes into my lungs – but today was a special day, and I figured my body was young and fit enough to take a pack of twenty B&H without dropping me with a coronary.

It felt good to be able to smoke openly on the street. My parents were gone for two weeks, and Greg Thatcher – the old guy from next door – had disappeared, too. My other neighbours were so reclusive that I was beginning to suspect they were really vampires. The only evidence of life was the red Sierra that appeared and disappeared mysteriously in the driveway. So nobody was going to see me smoking and tell my folks; for the rest of the fortnight, this was *my* house, and I could do in it what I liked. Just as long as I didn't leave any evidence that I'd done it.

"Alright, Danny," I said, raising my smouldering cigarette in salute.

"Alright, Jay," Danny replied. "Am I the first one here?"

"Yeah. The others should be turning up soon. Brought some beer, I see," I said, motioning to the clanking backpack that he was wearing.

Danny grinned. "I could've just bought some high-strength stuff, but *no*. I had to go and get twenty-four cans of the cheapest piss money can buy. Just about

2

herniated myself lugging them down from the shop. I'm holding my spine together by willpower alone; I reckon it's gonna give way as soon as I shed this lot." He shucked the backpack off and lowered it to the pavement. "Maybe not, then," he added, sounding almost disappointed. He took a few steps forward to check that he could still walk.

I watched him messing around on the pavement outside my house. Danny was a real character; my best friend, too. He was kind of short, with dirty-blond hair that wasn't really kept in any kind of style at all, but just left to go every which way. He was wearing huge, sand-coloured trousers, with a keychain arcing from his belt loop to his back pocket. His dark blue Etnies were almost buried under the ends of his trouser legs, and he was wearing an XL short-sleeved Dag Nasty T-shirt, with some kind of weird, ethereal face printed on it. I vaguely recalled hearing a Dag Nasty album last time I was round Danny's house; he loved his punk, did Danny. Never really rubbed off on me, though.

"Oh yeah, I forgot to tell you," I said. "Cathy rang earlier."

"She rang here?" asked Danny, then sighed. "What's the daft mare want now, then?"

I took a drag on my cigarette (I hate calling them *fags*; fags sound like a tramp's wet dog-end, not a classy line like B&H) and shrugged. "Probably checking to see if you got here okay or something."

Danny looked momentarily irritated, like he was going to get mad; but then he held up his hand as if to check himself. "Nope," he said. "I'm *not* gonna let her get on my nerves. Not tonight. Tonight is party night, right?"

"Right on, dude," I said, affecting a nasal California surfer drawl. We high-fived each other. We don't normally do stuff like that; we were sort of taking the piss. You know how it is. "Is Cathy coming, then?" I asked, swinging my legs on the wall, tapping my heels against the bricks.

Danny looked morose. "Yeah, worse luck. She'll do my head in all night, no doubt." He clapped his hands together and rubbed them. "I'll just have to get too plastered to understand her rabid warbling. That's the only way out of it." As if to compound this statement, he reached into his backpack for a can of beer.

"*Why* do you go out with her?" I asked him, for what must have been the millionth time.

True to form, Danny delivered the same answer he always did. "It's something to do." But I thought that it had to be more than that. You can't suffer the amount of grief that Cathy gave Danny without a better reason than *that*.

I let it drop, anyway. My mind was on other things. The party, for one. This party was to be a landmark in our lives, me and my friends. We had all ploughed our way through our GCSEs, with varying degrees of success, and were looking at a summer of fun ahead. No work, no strife, nothing but two solid months of *playtime*. But after that summer ... well, I didn't want to think about that right now. Like Danny said, tonight was party night.

Danny cracked his first beer while I finished my cigarette, and we sat out on that glorious summer evening and talked about a whole lot of nothing while we waited for the others to arrive. I nicked one of Danny's cans – "party tax," I explained cheekily – and we just kicked back and relaxed. The others would be here in their own sweet time.

"Is Jo Anderson coming?" Danny asked me suddenly. He said it like the thought had just occurred to him, but I could tell he'd been dying to ask for a while.

I felt a wry smile curl across my face. "*May*be she is," I said. "And *may*be she isn't.'

Danny laughed and poked me in the thigh. "She's coming? Alright! So you get your chance at last, yeah?"

I was playing it cagey. "We'll see," I said. I was, shall we say, quietly confident about the whole thing.

"I'm gonna be sorely disappointed if you don't pull her tonight, Jay," Danny teased. "You've been rattling on about her for so damn long, I don't think my ears could stand listening to you moaning about her all summer."

"Like I said, we'll see," I replied.

"But you *are* gonna go for it, yeah?"

I rubbed my hands together and cackled malevolently, playing the evil megalomaniac. "Once she has stepped into my lair, she is *mine*," I hissed, and Danny broke out into peals of laughter.

Truth was, I had fancied Jo Anderson for a long time. I didn't want to think about how long. She was in some of my classes at school, and I often saw her at lunchtimes. Sometimes we hung out together. Y'see, that was the problem with the whole thing. She was my friend. Not just some girl I knew, but one of my *friends*. And that meant I had to handle this *veeery* delicately indeed.

The thing with Jo was that we never saw each other outside school. See, the way people act towards each other at school is totally different to the way they act when they see each other in the pub, or whatever. At school, you can't do *anything* without it being amplified and reported by a hundred sneaky little gossiping spies. So people are more guarded. But the trouble was, outside of school, we just didn't go to the same places. She was always off to dance clubs, and they really aren't my thing.

So I never got to meet her where it counted, where people are easier and you can just hang out together. And I never got the chance to see if she really likes me. Likes me as more than a friend, I mean. This party was gonna be the last chance I got to see her before the summer, after which I was pretty sure I'd never see her again. We were going to different places next year for our A-levels. I was staying at school, she was going to college. So this was my last and only chance to make her my girlfriend.

I was sweating it a bit, I don't mind telling you.

The next to arrive was Sam Black, carrying a polythene bag bulging with a bottle of cheap vodka and a two-litre bottle of Virgin Cola. Me and Danny were still messing around out front when he arrived. It was one of his more bizarre entrances. We'd been expecting him to come walking up the road from the opposite direction to Danny, but instead we heard the click of a latch behind us and he came trolling out of my house, through the front door, like he owned the place. His usually immaculate hair was scruffy and mussed, his shoes were scuffed with dirt, but he just wandered up to us and said "Hi" like there was nothing unusual. It was just so weird that me and Danny split ourselves laughing.

"What the hell happened to you?" Danny asked.

Now to see me or Danny all messed-up and dirty is no big thing; but Sam is a label-head with a price tag on his wardrobe that could clear the Third World debt, and he has an image to maintain. When he arrived all dishevelled and sweaty, it seemed almost unreal.

"I came over through the Zone," Sam replied. "Dumb idea. The zombies are out early this evening. Walked right into a bunch of them."

"You came through the Zone? What for?" I asked.

"I couldn't get a lift over here, and I couldn't be bothered with the bus," he said. "Nearly got a good kicking for it, too. Anyway, I got chased out by some of 'em, and then I came in through your back garden. Your patio door's open. There was nobody in the house, so I figured you were out here."

The Zone was the generally accepted term for the old, derelict estate at the back of my street, across a few fields. It used to be a pretty nice place, with a few light-industry factories, offices and stuff, but some firebug torched it a while back and that was that. It had been due to be demolished for a long time, but nobody wanted the land, and I guess the council never got round to doing anything about it.

"I suppose it's been a while," Sam was saying. "I'd forgotten what that place was like. Hey, do you mind if I go inside and clean up a bit?"

"Sure," I said. I had expected him to ask, anyway. Couldn't have Sam Black looking a mess, could you? What would the *girls* think? He disappeared back inside.

"The *Zone*, bro!" Danny said, doing that California surfer thing again. "Dude, it's been, like, a *thousand* years since any of us set foot in there, man."

"Not since when Davey Roebuck sent us in," I said.

"Whoa, remember that one?" he replied, losing his accent in the excitement of the memory. "That was a finale and a half."

"You still got that keyring?" I asked.

Danny smiled slowly, reaching into his back pocket. Attached to the keychain at his belt was his wallet and his door keys, but hanging with them was a slim, teardrop-shaped brass keyring. He unclipped it and gave it to me.

I turned it over in my hand. On one side, the initials *I. H.* were carved into it. It was flat and unremarkable. But to me and Danny – and every other kid who had been Zone Running – this was like the Holy Grail. Ian Huntingdon's keyring.

It worked like this: each of the rival Zone-Running teams would dare the others into doing missions that were progressively more stupid and dangerous, until one of them failed or wussed out. When Davey Roebuck challenged us to steal Ian Huntingdon's keyring, we thought he'd gone just about far enough. Ian Huntingdon was a legend in the Zone. Not only did he have a questionable stake in the real world (whatever he was doing down in the Zone couldn't have been good for him), he was aggro as anything. And he *hated* Zone Runners.

I could still remember the feeling, cold and sick with fear but charged with excitement at the same time, as we crept into the NoGo area of the Zone. The blackened buildings crowded over us, their burned-out windows like dark eye sockets, watching us malevolently as we picked our way through the rubble-strewn alleys. My heart thrummed in my chest as the sounds of laughter, music and shouting drifted to us from the Square; because the laughter sounded evil to us, frightening. It came from the stoners, junkies and freaks who hung out in the Zone: the zombies. And we didn't like to think what they would do to us if they caught us Zone Running through their patch.

We skirted the edge of the Square, Danny in the lead, choosing out a path through the broken buildings that jutted up like crooked, crumbling teeth from the concrete gums of the Zone. We knew where Ian Huntingdon would be: right down there among the rest of the zombies. But we had prepared for our mission thoroughly. We had been down into the NoGo every night for the last week, observing, watching Ian's movements, planning how we could accomplish the mission that Davey Roebuck had set us.

And as we watched, we saw that there *was* a way.

In the end, only me and Danny had the guts to do it. Out on the far edge of the Square was the car lot. It wasn't a real car lot, just a broad slab of relatively rubble-free concrete which was open to the road; but that was where Ian left his car, hidden in the shadows.

There was a reason for that, of course. All sorts of ropey stuff had been going on with him and this new girl he'd acquired a few days ago. Every night, after Ian had finished getting whacked out on whatever was the substance of the day, he would lead her back to that car lot and they would climb into his car... you get the idea.

But this was *our* idea. What Ian was up to in that car meant he definitely didn't need his jeans, and his keys were in the pocket of his jeans, and on his keys was his keyring. Get it? Only one problem. One of us would have to reach right into the car to get them. And it would be a pretty fair bet that Ian wouldn't be happy about that.

So when we came back to the Zone on the night we decided to pull it off, we brought buckets. And on the way to the Square, we picked up all sorts of nasty stuff to put in them.

The mark of a good Zone Runner was forward planning. And we were pretty good.

We gave Ian and his girl a quarter of an hour in his

car before we struck. Our patience couldn't last any longer anyway. My nerves were twined up so tight I could hardly breathe. So we crept low towards the dark black shape of his Capri, under a clouded moon. The wind seemed to hiss through the teeth of the Zone buildings, a hollow warning of our approach. But Ian was too tied up to notice, I think, and it was just my imagination anyway.

I wasn't ready when Danny went ahead and did it. I was psyching myself up, thinking how was I ever gonna do what I had to do, and he just got sick of waiting. He yanked open the back door of the car, reached right in there and pulled out Ian's jeans. There was a shriek and a bellow of "Oi!" from inside, and then we were legging it across the tarmac, getting out of there while we still could.

Ian came running out, absolutely berserk with fury. But Sam was ready for him. He slung a bucket full of broken glass, sharp stones and bottle tops across the ground behind me and Danny. Ian was mad, but he wasn't wearing any shoes, and he wasn't stupid. Much.

The zombies mobbed in less than a minute, heading off in the direction we had gone, baying for our blood. When they saw the torchlight flashing in the empty window of the old aluminium can factory, they thought they had us; but all they found was a lonely torch, hanging by a piece of string from a beam, dancing in the wind. We had doubled back and left them for dead.

The keyring that I held in my hand represented our

last run. We had not only stolen Ian's keyring, *and* his jeans, but we had escaped the Zone without being recognized. We were never going to top that, and nobody else could either.

But then the new school term had started, and the thrill and fame had jaded a little after a while. And us Runners began to realize that the older kids weren't interested in catching us and beating us up, but were content to ignore our daring forays and sniff Bri-Wax instead. And so we had wound down our illustrious career as Zone Runners, and began to think of other things, like school and girls.

I closed my hand around the keyring and gave it back to Danny. "I kinda think sometimes we shouldn't have stopped," I said. "It was such a damn good laugh."

"They were good days," Danny agreed sagely, and I knew that he'd been thinking just the same as me.

Chapter Two

Cappo turned up not long afterwards. His real name was Neil, Neil Capley; but you know how it goes with surnames. Anyway, we were still sitting on the porch, watching the sun on its slow descent, when his dad's Peugeot pulled up and he got out. I noted with relief that I didn't have a tab on the go at the time; Cappo's dad and mine sometimes played golf together, and though he's quite cool about stuff like that, I wouldn't want to risk getting caught.

Cappo pulled his schoolbag out of the car and swung it on to his shoulder. His dad wanted to talk to him a bit before he went, and Cappo listened with an expression on his face like he didn't care what his dad was saying. Then he shut the passenger door – not gently – and walked over to us. His dad watched him for a minute and then drove off; I couldn't see his expression because of the glare of the sun on the windscreen.

Now I'm usually the last person to ask when it comes to people's feelings – I'm invariably wrong about who fancies who, and when people are depressed I think they're just pissed off, and so on – but even I could tell that Cappo was mad with his dad about something. They were usually quite a close family. I'd been over there a few times.

To look at Cappo, you'd think he wasn't anything special. He had a face that was too narrow, a jaw that was a little too pronounced, and short dark hair that didn't do much to flatter him. His gear wasn't much to write home about either; he never wore anything particularly extravagant, all middle-of-the-road kind of stuff, Sweater Shop and Levi's. But it was just a case of crappy wrapping paper, really. Not only was he an absolutely diamond guy, he was a *to*tal genius as well. You know, one of those people that really makes you sick because they're good at everything without even really trying. It was a safe bet that if any of us had aced their GCSEs, it was Cappo. On top of that, he couldn't half rip on the piano – he knew practically everything by the Prodigy – and he was a pretty dab hand at the guitar, too. Music was one of his GCSEs. The teacher, Mr Hurney, had already virtually promised him an A.

If it had been anybody else, I might have been a little jealous of his talent. He was a guy for whom everything seemed to turn out right. But Cappo was way too nice for jealousy; I reckoned he deserved everything he had. I reached into Danny's bag to offer him a welcome beer. Danny wasn't having any of that, though, and he yanked the drawstring so the bag closed tight around my hand.

"Uh-uh," he said.

I freed my hand from the trap. I still had half a beer in my other hand, so I offered that to Cappo instead.

"S'okay, I've got my own," said Cappo, patting his bag. "How're you guys, anyway?"

14

"Not bad," replied Danny.

"Thought I'd get here early," he said. "Carve myself out a place on the floor before it's overrun by everyone else."

"I dunno if it's gonna be *that* packed," I said. "I didn't invite any of the crazies; I didn't want this thing to get out of hand."

"How many do you reckon are coming?"

"Forty, fifty maybe. Enough..." I began.

"But not *too* many," Danny finished for me.

"Does Stew and that lot know about it?" Cappo asked, referring to the group of dropout retard towny bully-boys that comprised most of class 11B.

"I hope to hell not," I replied. I knew what they were like when they were drunk, and I also had a keen sense of the value of most of my household ornaments. Besides, they were vicious sons of bitches. Most of them didn't give a damn about anything. What a bunch. Laugh a minute. I mean, don't get me wrong, it's not like they bully me or anything. That's not why I hate them; in fact I'm pretty civil to most of them. It's just that they're all about who's the hardest, who can hurt the other guy more, and I'm not into that.

I thought over what Cappo had said about Stew and the party and I really began to get a little disturbed by the idea. Anything Cappo said – even a backhanded suggestion like that one – had an unnerving habit of turning out to be right. I hoped that this time was an exception.

*   *   *

Now the four of us were here, the real stalwarts. Me, Danny, Cappo and Sam, we were the hard core of our group of friends. Every lunchtime we'd meet at the stairs by the science block, and we'd hang around together, finding stuff to do or just having a laugh. Occasionally we were divided by girlfriends (Danny had a longstanding thing going with Cathy, like I said, and Sam went through women like a stone through wet kitchen roll) but we would always return to the fold in the end. These guys were my real friends.

Which brings me to the other problem, and the other reason for this party. I've already told you that this thing was a) a celebration and b) a chance to get my slimy claws on Jo Anderson – well, now for c)...

St Paul's School, where we all went until recently, was on one side of town. Fenimore College was *waaay* over the other side. This was the situation as it stood, GCSE grades allowing: I was staying on at St Paul's, to get my A-Levels (with luck). Cappo was definitely staying on, because like I said, he was a genius. Danny, on the other hand, was wandering off to Fenimore at the end of the summer, because they did a Psychology course and he was into all that mind-twisting stuff. Sam, who had never been very motivated at school anyway, was dropping out to work for his dad in the interior decorating business.

I didn't want to lose Danny and Sam. But I had a horrible feeling that I wouldn't see them again. It happens, y'see. People drift apart. Danny would make other friends at college, people whom I didn't know, and who were probably infinitely more exciting than most of the saps at St Paul's. Sam would lose touch, working all the time and having less and less in common with us, as he took the working-man route and we stayed in education. I knew it was a little silly, that we'd still see each other outside school; but I could just see those meetings becoming less and less frequent, until eventually, we gave up making the effort to be friends.

So, that was what this party was about. Reason c): I wanted memories, I wanted us to have some good times together while we could, because these guys were my best friends ever, and even I know that's a precious thing. And maybe I wanted to try and prevent the inevitable, and keep us all from drifting apart. How I was gonna do that, I had *no* idea.

Sam came downstairs and we went into the lounge. We'd moved inside shortly after Cappo had arrived, because there was only space on my wall for two of us to sit and nobody fancied sitting on the skanky pavement.

My lounge is a pretty typical affair, with a real stone fireplace, white plaster walls and a lime-coloured carpet. The furniture – which is a different shade of green – is all matched, and pretty plush with it. The armchairs and sofa are covered in some sort of velvety stuff which lets you work up some awesome static on it and zap your friends.

"So how'd you get on with that girl on Friday?" Danny asked Sam, with a mischievous tint to his words.

Sam looked momentarily bemused, an expression

of confusion crossing his face. It was, I sicken to admit, what you might call *ruggedly handsome*; he already had a full cheekload of thick stubble, clear skin and good-looking features, topped off with grape-green eyes that women died for on a regular basis. "Friday?" he said.

"You know," Danny prompted. "Blonde hair? Black top? No?"

We all knew what he was talking about. We'd gone out to the local nightclub – Tito's – on Friday after a bit of a pub crawl. Sam had disappeared soon after we got in there (this is his *modus operandi*, I reckon; we must cramp his style) and was seen later necking with some girl who we didn't know. She looked at least eighteen, though, which was pretty good going for Sam, who was sixteen like the rest of us.

"Oh yeah, I know who you mean," Sam said.

"You seen her since?" asked Danny.

Sam made a sort of dismissive noise. "Nah," he said. "Didn't have two brain cells to knock together. Good for a few hours, but after that..."

Danny thought this was a riot. Maybe it was something in the way Sam said it. We were all used to the way Sam treated girls, and none of us were moralistic enough to raise an objection to his attitude. If you got it, use it, that's what I say. Probably because I haven't got it. Sam, unlike Cappo, is someone I could get healthily jealous of at times.

We cracked a few more cans, and me and Sam smoked some tabs. He had a twenty-pack of Death cigarettes, which he said he bought "because they had a cool skull-and-crossbones thing on the filter". I ask you – Death cigarettes. Like we need to be reminded.

Sam talked about the football a bit, but me and Danny don't really follow it and Cappo – who was a fairweather supporter of whichever team were at the top of the league at the time – didn't seem to have much interest today. He dipped into his schoolbag, and for a moment I caught a glimpse of just how much alcohol he had in there. Lager, spirits, a bottle of wine. . . what, was he planning to share them out or something? All I knew was, I had a healthy respect for how much Cappo could drink, but the amount he was lugging could put a grizzly under. I was going to say something, but other people were talking and I didn't really want to interrupt. In the end, the whole thing just drifted out of my mind.

"How are you and Cathy getting along?" Sam asked Danny. "I haven't seen her for ages."

I groaned mentally. Mentioning her wasn't a good idea. It always got Danny started. He surprised me, though, and was remarkably suppressed. Usually Cathy is just about the only thing that can get him worked up. "Ah, she's moaning at me about going on holiday to Spain."

"What, she wants you to go with her?"

"No, she doesn't want me to go. With my parents. She reckons she'll miss me for two weeks. Thing is, she's got a job doing packing at a factory over the summer, two in the afternoon till ten at night, so I'm never gonna see her anyway, except at weekends."

"Wanna bet that she'll be too tired then to go out?" I said, putting my tuppence-worth in.

Danny conceded this with a shrug. "I wouldn't be surprised."

"And she's hacking you for *that*?" said Sam. "It's not like you can tell your parents you're not going, is it?"

Danny agreed wholeheartedly. "Exactly," he said. "Tickets have been booked and so on. But she's still on at me: '*Don't go, don't go.*'" He mimicked her cruelly in a whiny voice. "I swear, if she had a problem with the sun coming up in the morning she'd moan at me until I fixed it."

"Poke her eyes out with a stick," I suggested helpfully.

Danny appeared to give this some thought. "Not bad," he said eventually. "But messy."

"There's no sense in 'em, I swear," Sam agreed. "I had the same thing happen to me, with—"

"Guys and girls just *aren't* going to get along," said Cappo suddenly. There was something unusual about the way he said it, like a little bit hard-edged. And it was doubly unusual that he had interrupted Sam, especially since he'd been a bit quiet ever since he turned up. I put it down to the residual bad vibes from whatever disagreement he'd had with his dad. "They're built differently, they *think* differently. Cathy probably thinks you're just being a stubborn asshole 'cause you'd rather go on holiday with your parents than her. I bet she hasn't even thought through the practicalities of it."

"Gee, thanks," Danny said, jokingly.

Cappo didn't reciprocate the humour. "I mean, you and Cathy, yeah? You argue all the time. *All* the time."

"That's because she's dozy," said Danny, with unassailable logic.

"Or because she doesn't understand you. And you don't understand her. Male and female brains work differently, that's a fact. It's—"

"Whoa, can we tone it down a bit?" I said. Cappo had been getting a little worked up about the whole thing. *Triply* unusual, that was, because he was normally so calm. "This is gonna be a party. Leave the hefty battle-of-the-sexes stuff outside, okay?"

Cappo looked at me levelly. "I just get a bit sick of people going on about girl problems when everybody knows that us and them'll never get along."

Danny was too bemused by this pronouncement to bother rising to the insinuation – that Cappo was tired of hearing about Cathy. I changed the subject with my usual skill, and pretty soon the whole thing had been forgotten by everyone.

At least, I hoped it had.

Chapter Three

By about eight o'clock, people had begun to arrive. The lounge was first to fill up, as that was where the centre of activity was; but it soon became too full and people started splitting up into groups. Kerry Macclesfield and her cronies – who were kind of my childhood friends from the street and whom I was virtually obligated to invite even though I didn't really like them any more – got an early start on dominating the kitchen. They could be relied on to guard the beers in the fridge without nicking any. A couple of Castaways and they were anybody's; they wouldn't need to steal extra beer. Not that anybody actually *wanted* Kerry and Co. unless they were blitzed and with beer goggles firmly attached, but that was another story.

The lounge was filled with the soft sounds of the new Orbital album. Danny had brought some albums to put on, but I gently pointed out that nobody except him would like that kind of music. Danny, as I said before, was well into his West Coast punk. I could take it or leave it, myself. But, being the gracious host, I had to put the needs of the many before the needs of the few, and Orbital was good background music as far as I was concerned.

I waved hello to Cathy as she appeared at the door to the lounge, popping her head round. She was a fairly good-looking girl – not really my sort, though – with shoulder-length, copper-red hair in curls. A smattering of freckles was airbrushed across the bridge of her uptilted nose, and as she stepped into the room, I saw that she was wearing a long, summery floral dress that hugged her gorgeous figure *aaaaall* the way down.

She smiled waifishly at me in acknowledgement before fixing her eyes on Danny, who was sitting next to me, studying his can of Viborg. Unable to meet his eyes, she instead began picking her way through the knots of people who were sitting around the floor of the lounge in clusters, smoking and boozing.

"Incoming," I murmured to Danny out of the corner of my mouth. He looked up in surprise – though I thought he'd been ignoring Cathy, he genuinely hadn't seen her – and smiled warmly as she sat down next to him, arranging her curls over her creamy-white shoulders.

"Hi," she said. She had a honey-smooth voice. You wouldn't suspect that under that innocent, fresh-faced girl's skin was a maniacal whirlwind of female hormones.

"Alright, Cath," I said. She slipped a possessive arm around Danny's shoulder. "I thought you didn't get off work till ten."

"Oh, I don't start at the factory until next week," she said. "No, I was round Helen's house, and I got a lift here with her parents."

"Helen Cowley?" I asked. Helen Cowley was Stew's girlfriend. Her and Cathy were occasional friends, when their boyfriends weren't at odds with each other. Unlike me, Danny wasted no effort concealing his dislike of Stew and Co.

"Yeah, that's right."

"I didn't know she was coming," I said. Meaning: I didn't *invite* her, I don't *like* her, what the hell is she *doing* here? I can whack a good deal of subtext into very few words, believe you me.

Cathy got the gist. She turned apologetic on me. "She's just broke up with Stew," she said. "She was going to go with them down to the Zone tonight, but she had an argument, so I invited her along. You don't mind, do you?"

I couldn't very well turf her out, could I? "No, it's alright by me," I said grudgingly.

"They're going down to the Zone?" asked Danny.

"They're having a celebration of their own," Cathy explained. "An end-of-exams booze-up. They're camping out in the Zone."

Danny blew his lips derisively. "Rather them than me. Why sit here in the warm when you can spend the night in a place that makes the surface of the Moon look cheery?"

Cathy giggled on cue, but Danny's words had provoked a nasty suspicion in me. "Did Helen mention if Stew knew about this party?"

"She didn't say," said Cathy, "but he wouldn't come if he did. He's got his own party."

I felt a weight lift from my shoulders (metaphorically, of course; you never actually *feel* it) and allowed myself a small smile of satisfaction. Stew was out of the picture; that was one less thing to worry about.

Well, once Cathy had turned up I knew that I could pretty much give up trying to talk to Danny. She monopolized his time ruthlessly, constantly engaging him in conversation and butting in whenever he tried to talk to somebody else. She wasn't rude, she just had this ... *way* of steering a conversation so that it always revolved around her. Anyhow, I shuffled over and sat nearer to Cappo and Sam, who were both silently watching people arrive.

Sam saw me moving away from Danny and began to natter to me with an expression of what might have been relief on his face. I got the impression that Cappo hadn't been talking much, and their conversation had got a little strained. Unfortunately, we were still too close to him to discuss it, so we talked about other stuff instead. Just general taking-the-piss stuff, nothing of any real gravity.

I was well into my third beer now, and it was going down smoothly. Everything was looking pretty rosy from my point of view. The party was beginning to swing, people were obviously enjoying themselves ... but there was just one thing. It was approaching eight-thirty, a full hour after the party officially started, and there was still no sign of Jo Anderson. Not that this worried me; I reckoned people would still be turning up till around ten. But I really began to hope that she wouldn't decide to go to some dance club instead. I'd psyched myself up so much about tonight, I didn't know what I'd do if she didn't show.

Me and Sam decided to check out the back garden, as the sun was going in now and it was cooling off a bit. I asked Cappo if he was coming, but he said no and cracked open another can. So we weaved through the little clusters of people who had planted themselves in my living room floor, and I slid open the big patio door that opened out on to the back garden.

My garden was a two-storey thing, pretty flash by most people's standards, but then my dad always liked a spot to stretch out and relax in so he'd insisted on a big garden when he bought the house. The lower section was all paved, with a couple of round white tables with collapsed parasols in the centre. Around these were supposed to be a load of plastic chairs, but they'd already been filched and moved around by the partygoers, so they were now scattered all over the place. From the lower section, a couple of steps ran up to the lawn, which was wide and flat and stretched back into a little grove of trees. Beyond that was a strip of fields, and beyond *that* ... the Zone.

You couldn't actually see the Zone from my house. It was hidden behind a rise in the land. Presumably that was why nobody had ever bothered knocking it down; it was out of sight and out of mind. But tonight, it kind of got to me. I don't know why. Maybe it was because me and Danny had been talking about Ian Huntingdon. I imagined that it was crouching there, just waiting, waiting for something. Like all the charred buildings had turned their blank window-eyes to look at me.

Oh, will you *listen* to yourself? I thought. I shook myself back into the real world.

Six or seven people were milling around in the lower, paved section, smoking tabs and drinking. I recognized most of them, and me and Sam went over to say hello to Rich, who was there with his girlfriend. Rich is unofficially known as Thunderchunk (unofficially in that you don't say it to his face if you like how your own looks) on account of his huge size. He's not fat, or muscly, but is he ever *beefy*. Anyway, me and him were on pretty good terms, we got along well. I think I had one of his Aphex Twin CDs in my bedroom at the time, but I reckoned he'd forgotten about it by now, so I decided not to mention it if he didn't.

"Howya doin'?" said Thunderch... Rich. "Nice house."

"So far," I replied impishly.

"Yeah, we'll see how it looks when this is all over," said Sam with a grin.

With three beers inside me, I was too laid-back to let that worry me. I looked up at the last sunlight in the sky and felt okay.

"Who's this?" Sam asked Rich, turning his attention to Rich's girlfriend, who was looking at her shoes, obviously a little intimidated by all the people she didn't know. She was a willowy girl with pretty blonde plaits, and one of those interesting faces that wasn't quite attractive but which I could have spent hours looking at.

"I'm Gemma," she said coyly, almost visibly melting when she saw Sam. Sam favoured her with one of his most dazzlingly demure smiles.

"This is Sam and Jay," Rich said, motioning to Sam and me in turn. She barely gave me a cursory glance before returning her attention to Sam, doe-eyed with admiration. I swear, I don't know how he does it. Inwardly, I prayed that he wouldn't be stupid enough to be tempted by her; Sam was a pretty tough customer, but Thunderchunk would pulp him if it came to that. And though it might sound slack to you, I really wouldn't put it past Sam to nick someone's girlfriend behind their back. Where girls were concerned, the guy had no morals whatsoever.

I decided to lead him away before he could get tempted. We went back through the kitchen way, past a couple of guys I knew from my class who were rolling up on the back doorstep. Kerry Macclesfield was sitting up on the breakfast bar, swinging her stockinged feet, with a bottle of Castaway (I hate to say *I told you so*, but...) in her hand and a cigarette between her lips. She was a tall girl, leaning towards bony, and without sugar-coating it, she was something of a moose.

Don't think me shallow; I know a lot of ugly girls who are a great laugh. But Kerry, well, she put it about a bit. She had something of a reputation for being easy, which was complicated by the fact that nobody fancied her when they were sober. When you were drunk, though ... it was a whole new ball game.

Sam had pulled her before when he was blitzed; he's never lived it down, bless him.

Kerry's friends appeared to have deserted her, so I had a quick chat with her about nothing in particular. Sam shuffled around in the background, looking embarrassed, while Kerry fixed him with a predatory eye. I was midway through a sentence when I heard the doorbell ring. I had a clear view down the hall to the front door, and though the semi-opaque glass meant that I could only see a blurred outline of who was outside, I had a virtual premonition of who it must be.

" 'Scuse me," I said, and left Sam to Kerry while I made my way to the door before anybody else could open it. The hall was relatively empty, so I didn't have to rush, but by the time I got to the door, my heart was hammering as if I'd run a mile.

I opened the door, and there was Jo Anderson. It was the first time – excepting school own-clothes days – that I'd seen her in anything other than the disfiguring St Paul's uniform. She looked unbelievable. Slim, pretty, hair in a loose bob around a heart-shaped face; this girl was my personal idea of perfection. Along with her dark-crimson trousers, she was wearing a tight white T-shirt with a stylized Japanese cartoon spaceman printed on it, winking cutely through his open visor.

"Hi, Jo!" I said brightly. "Come in!"

She beamed at me in the failing light and stepped over the threshold into my house. She was carrying a bottle of wine. Nice one, I thought, she's gonna get drunk. That made my job much easier.

"That's a cool T-shirt," I said. It was something that I might have said to anyone, but when I said it to her is sounded like a thuddingly clumsy line.

"Cheers," she said, sounding genuine. "I got it from Undertones; they were having a sale."

"Looks good," I said, admiring the motif and the swell of her breasts beneath it. The spidery outline of her white bra was just visible beneath the fabric; but I could hardly let my gaze linger there, much as it wanted to.

"You staying here the night?" I asked, knowing that she lived a considerable distance away (another reason why I never saw her much).

"Yeah, I'm getting picked up tomorrow," she purred. "That's okay, isn't it?"

"Course, no problem," I replied swiftly. Inside, I was rejoicing. That gave me all night to work on her.

I realized that we were standing alone in the hallway, and suddenly I couldn't think of anything else to say to her. "Come into the lounge," I said, before the silence could become long enough to be embarrassing.

"Sure, thanks," she said. I closed the door behind her and led the way into the lounge, where I hoped my spot on the floor had not been stolen. Miraculously, there was still an empty space next to Cappo, between him and the combined organism of Danny and Cathy.

Jo helloed a few people as we crossed the room (which was beginning to get cosily stuffy now). Most of the people here were my friends and not hers, but she knew enough people to get by. It hadn't been planned, but it was a fortunate happenstance; as she didn't have many good friends here, she was less likely to wander away with someone else. I wanted her to myself tonight.

We sat down next to Cappo, who responded to my greeting with a barely discernible grunt from the depths of his beer can. I was a little put out; I'd never known him to be this uncommunicative. But right now I didn't have time to sympathize with him, because Jo was nestling into a spot next to me. Her hand brushed down my arm as she settled herself; it tingled with the pleasant memory of her touch for a few seconds afterwards.

We chatted for a bit, making small talk, messing around a bit, having a laugh. After we had been going for a while, I decided to attempt that tricky manoeuvre: introducing something important into a conversation.

"It's weird, isn't it?" I said, voicing what I had been thinking all evening. "I mean, this must be the first time we've ever, like, been out together." My words sounded stupid to me, but I'd pretty much resigned myself to the fact that everything I said to Jo this evening was going to make me sound like a moron.

"We're not really *out*, are we?" she said, waving a hand around my lounge.

"You know what I mean," I said.

"Yeah, I know. I dunno, maybe it's just because we live too far apart. I guess we should have, really."

"We have a laugh in our English classes, don't we?"

Jo grinned. "Yeah, we do." She looked around a bit, and then took a swig from her bottle of wine. It was only then that I noticed it had already been uncorked, and was one-third empty. Cool.

I burrowed behind an armchair for my own bag of drinks and got myself a can. I know it was my house, but at parties it's a lot safer to keep those drinks safely stashed in a bag and hidden someplace than left in the fridge. Around eleven, when most people's beer starts to run out, they suddenly realize that they haven't bought enough. So they take whatever beer's in the fridge; it doesn't matter whose. I cracked it open and took a swallow.

"Maybe we should get together over the summer sometime," I said. Whoops, too fast, should've left it a bit, let the conversation get really flowing...

"Yeah," she said, with a smile that incinerated my insides. "That'd be cool. We should do."

Al*right*.

Chapter Four

The evening wore on and, Cappo aside, everything was going brilliantly. Danny and Cathy had wandered off somewhere, hand in hand. Sam was over the other side of the room, applying his charms to Anita Vernon. And me and Jo were getting on like the proverbial house on fire. What amazed me was that she hadn't even exhibited any desire to talk to anyone else; to the virtual exclusion of everyone, we were just talking to each other. I began to allow myself to really hope, to think: *maybe this is it.*

First rule of Life, the Universe and Everything: never admit to yourself that everything's going well. That's always the point when it starts to go wrong. And hey, who am I to buck the cosmic balance?

"Jay," called a voice on the other side of the room. It was Pete Baker, a gangly, acne-pocked kid who sat next to me in IT classes. He was okay, but he grated on your nerves a bit when you talked to him for too long. A bit *too* enthusiastic about his Star Trek and Babylon 5, if you see what I mean.

I looked up at him. He was standing by the door to the hallway, his face serious. "Trouble," he said. "You'd better come."

I glanced apologetically at Jo and got up. Half the room followed my example; they had heard Pete's announcement, and wanted to see what was going on. Jo came with me as I pushed my way through to the front door and was led outside by Pete.

It was dark now, but the sky was clear, and the stars studded the night with awesome luminescence. The moon was nowhere to be seen, but the streetlights had turned on and were washing the street in a greeny-yellow glow. I reckoned it was about ten o'clock, but I wasn't sure. I'd been drinking quite slowly while I'd been talking to Jo, but even so I was five or six cans under now, and I really didn't give a damn about the time.

I could hear what the problem was as soon as I stepped outside. Someone was bawling at the top of their voice somewhere close by.

"Helen! Oi, Helen! I know you're in there! Come out 'n' talk to me!"

Me and Pete exchanged glances. It was Stew.

I went out into my front garden and looked down the street. Stew was there, alone, with a bottle of what was probably whisky in his hand. He was yelling at the houses on my side of the road, stumbling drunkenly, shouting to each one as he went along. He was obviously looking for my house, but he didn't know exactly which one it was. He was making a hell of a racket; I glanced nervously at the houses on either side of the road, and saw faces in some of the windows, glaring balefully at him.

I leaned back behind the protective cover of the

hedge that divided my property from my neighbour's. "Damn," I muttered.

"You can't let him in here," said Pete urgently. "He's well aggro about something!"

"Someone's gonna call the police if we don't shut him up," I hissed. "And how much under-age drinking do you think is going on in my house? *How* much do I hate Helen Cowley?"

With that, I stepped out into the street. "Stew!" I called. "Quieten down! We're over here."

"Jay!" he called at equal volume. "Mate! How are you?" He began to stagger down the hill towards me.

Urrgh. If there's anything I hate more than rowdy drunks, it's friendly ones. I don't just mean friendly, I mean *friendly*. The ones who sling their arm roughly around your shoulder and stick their faces right next to yours, then tell you on a wave of beer breath how much of a great buddy you are and how much they love you.

"Keep it down, Stew!" I said. "I've got neighbours."

The faces at the window had all turned to look at me, as if I was responsible for this dickhead. I dreaded to think what would happen if any of them got indignant enough to call my parents when they returned. Or the police.

Stew, upon hearing my plea for quiet, laid a finger on his lips with a loud "*Sssssshhhh!*" and tiptoed exaggeratedly down the street towards me, swaying wildly between the kerb and the garden walls on my side of the road.

I leaned back to where Pete was waiting, like a right-hand man. "Go and get Helen Cowley. Tell her what's up." Pete nodded and rushed into the house. Jo was watching me from the front door of my house, other faces crowding round her. The eyes of my party guests were on me. I was feeling a little nervous, but then again I was feeling pretty drunk as well, which meant I was just about invulnerable.

"Jay, mate? Where –" Stew began, at the top of his lungs again. I thanked my lucky stars (assuming I have some) that my neighbours were away. He'd obviously lost his way as soon as I had disappeared out of sight. Idiot. I popped back out on to the pavement hastily.

"Over here, Stew," I said quickly. An expression of comic enlightenment dawned on his face and he carried on stumbling.

Stew was a tall kid, with fairly broad shoulders even though his arms were thin. He wasn't massively big and strong – I flattered myself that I could hold him to a standstill in a fight – but he was awfully aggressive, and that intimidated a lot of people, me included. It was hard to relax around someone that might suddenly batter you for no reason.

He had centre-parted, blond hair, hanging down to the top of his ears, and he wore an earring with a cross dangling from it. I had never asked him, but I doubted the cross had any Christian significance. He was wearing a black puffer jacket – which he'd had for years, after he nicked it from some kid at a music recital at school – over an Adidas sweater, and he had on a pair of scuffed Lee jeans and a set of manky Nikes. Right now he looked a state; really, really gone. Slobberingly drunk. If he was looking for Helen, I was sure that she'd just *love* to see him like this.

He stumbled into my front garden, and cast a bleary eye around all the faces that watched him from the front door and the lounge windows. "You didn't tell us you were having a party," he slurred.

"I didn't think you'd want to come," I lied smoothly. "I heard that you were having a party of your own in the Zone."

Stew leered. "Ha. Yeah. We got ... we got a bonfire 'n' everything."

I waited for him to go on. He had something to say, but at the moment he looked too pissed to recall what it was. I looked at the bottle in his hand. Yup, whisky.

I was facing him alone. I sure as hell wasn't going to let him into my house in the state that he was in, and everybody else was content to watch the drama from inside. Only I stood, halfway up my garden path, between Stew and my party. On the one hand, I felt well cool, standing there like that, the lone defender. On the other, I was *so* apprehensive about what Stew was going to do next.

After a few moments, he fixed me with an unfocused eye. "You got Helen in there, haven'tcha?"

I considered denying it for a second, but it probably wasn't a good idea. I'd already sent Pete to get her. "Yeah, I think so."

"Good. I knew that. Cathy's mum told me," he said. "See . . . see, I wanna talk to her, see."

I didn't really know what to say. I couldn't let him in, but I didn't want to tell him that. And until Helen got here (where *was* she, anyway?), he couldn't speak to her.

"Me 'n' her had a fight," he said, after a short silence. "Just wanna see her, straighten things out. Make up with her, yeah?" He grabbed me by the shoulders. "She's a fox, yeah?"

"Who, Helen?" I didn't like him touching me.

"Helen. I'm lucky to have her, yeah?" His eyes were focusing and unfocusing disconcertingly, and his jaw was slack.

"She's a nice girl," I said evasively. Was she hell. I would have cheerfully given her a slap if she'd been there. I *knew* it'd be trouble when Cathy brought her here. Well, actually, that's a lie; I had no idea. But it made me feel better thinking it. And I wouldn't *really* slap her. Maybe.

"She is," he said, then his eyes fixed on something over my shoulder. "Helen!" he called.

Helen was shepherded out of the doorway by Pete. She was a small, mousy girl, with spectacles and black hair tied back in a tight ponytail. She looked pityingly at her boyfriend as she came over to him. I backed off a bit, both to give them space and to surreptitiously guard the entrance to my house. Pete took up position next to me.

"Nice one, Pete," I said out of the corner of my mouth. "Good timing."

Pete grinned.

"Helen," Stew was dribbling. "Helen, I'm sorry, Helen." He was trying to put his arms round her, but she was having none of it. She kept on pushing his hands away.

"Stewart, you're drunk," she said accusingly. "What are you doing here?"

"Came to say I'm sorry, tha'ss all," Stew replied. I wished that I had a video camera to record this tender reunion. "To say ... I love you, Helen."

"You don't *love* me," said Helen, like she was scolding a child who didn't know what he meant. Which I thought, at the time, was a pretty accurate description of Stew.

"I do, I do," he gurgled. "Come back with me, Helen. The party's no fun without'cha."

"You should have thought of that before you started on me," Helen returned.

"But I didn't mean—"

"No, Stew," she continued, flattening his argument. "I've had it with you! How can I go out with someone who can't control their temper? You call me every name under the sun when you're mad, and you expect to say sorry and be forgiven? Sorry, but no way!"

Helen was pretty impressive when she was angry. The crowd were loving the spectacle. This whole Stew thing could turn out to be alright, I thought. It was a laugh to see him get stomped on by a girl that was a clear foot smaller than him.

"How c'n you say that, Helen? You ... you mean –"

"– everything to you, yes, I know," she said sarcastically. "You can't treat me like that and expect me to forgive you, Stew. Certainly not when you're drunk. You're only sorry because you're pissed and horny" – this raised a cheer from the assembled lads – "but in the morning you'll be just the same. Not this time, though. I've given you too many chances."

Stew was reeling under this verbal barrage. Probably he couldn't understand all the long words Helen was using ("and" and "to") but more likely he was processing the implications of what she had just said to him. It took him a while. Helen got in a suckerpunch while we were waiting.

"And look at the state you're in! You're a drooling mess!"

The guys in the doorway cheered again. Helen wheeled round and snapped at them to shut up, which only made them more rowdy.

"Helen, jus' come with me. I'll make it up to you, I promise."

"You haven't been listening to a word I've said, have you?" she replied. "This is it! We're not getting back together this time. No way."

"Give it some, Helen!" someone shouted.

"What you saying?" Stew slurred.

"Oh, sod it," said Helen, throwing her hands up in exasperation. "It's over, Stewart. Don't try to follow me, or call me, or anything. That's it."

With that, she swept past me and back into the house. My house. The realization struck me almost as soon as she left; she was sheltering in *my* house!

"Get back out here!" said Stew, suddenly angry, pushing to follow her. But I stopped him.

"You can't go in there, Stew," I said. While my voice was, I like to think, pretty stable, my legs were turning to jelly.

"What?" said Stew, looking at me in stupefied amazement. "Why not?"

"You're too drunk," I said. "And that's my parents' house."

"Get out of my way," he said, trying to shove me aside. But he didn't have any strength behind his effort and I pushed him off me. I knew then, with that terrible clarity you get when you've just done something you can't take back, that I had just started a fight. Like I said, he was an aggro kid. What I saw as basic self-defence, he would see as a challenge. I had pushed him.

Sure enough, his eyes, which had previously looked on me with a sickening mateyness, took on a glint of anger. "Tha'ss my girlfriend in there. I wanna go in 'n' see her," he said.

"You can't go in," I repeated. "Whatever's happening with you and her, I'm not letting you in my house. You're too pissed, and you'll wreck something. Talk to her out here."

"Get her out then. Lemme see her."

I was acutely aware of the eyes of the others on me, Jo included. Despite the fact that I didn't particularly like Helen, I couldn't very well throw her out of my party; especially after I told Cathy it was alright for her to be here. And I knew that she wouldn't come out of her own accord.

"I can't make her come out unless she wants to talk to you," I said. My blood was pounding in anticipation of the fight that I knew must come. I felt the heat in my face. I didn't want it, didn't want to fight, but I knew Stew wouldn't let this go.

"Helen!" he shouted again at the top of his voice. There was no reply. "I'm going in there," he said, trying to shove me out of the way again. Again, I stood my ground. His jaw became hard as he saw that I wasn't going to move.

"What are you *doing*, huh?" he said, pushing me hard on the shoulders. I took a step back. "You trying to protect her, or what? She's *my* girlfriend." He pushed me again. I'm not a violent person, but I didn't like that. Not at all.

"You," I said, shoving him hard, "*don't* bring *your* problems to *my* party." He stumbled backwards, too drunk to regain his balance, and fell over full-length on the grass of my front lawn. Shit, was he mad now!

Then there was another person beside me, instead of Pete (who had disappeared as soon as the confrontation started). "Got a problem, Jay?"

It was Sam. I was relieved that he was here, but I didn't let it show on my face. I just kept right on glaring at Stew, who was glaring back at me. I knew that something had started here that was not going to be soon forgotten, and the thought scared me a bit when I recalled it afterwards. But at the time, I was drunk and feeling angry, and all I was thinking was what he was gonna do next.

He got to his feet, almost falling back down once,

and looked from me to Sam to me again. Maybe he could take on one of us. Not both. Even he knew that.

Then he turned and left. That was it. No parting comment, no kamikaze attack; he just blundered off, pausing only to kick my garden wall (which probably hurt him more than it did the wall) and was gone.

I looked at Sam and nodded my gratitude. He was a good guy to back you up in a situation like that.

We waited for a few moments to see if Stew would come back, but he seemed gone for good. Then we turned around and made our way back inside. We'd done well, me especially. Some people patted my back as I slipped through the hallway. Jo looked a little worried, as my face must have shown how pissed off I was. I was heading up the stairs, the way Helen had gone. I had to have a few words with her.

Beneath me, the group in the hall began to disperse and drift away, chattering excitedly. I didn't see where Jo went, but I was glad she wasn't with me. The comedown from the excitement of a near-fight had left me in a bit of a mood, and I was going to take it out on the girl who deserved it most. I didn't want anyone else to see it, especially not Jo.

Helen was in the spare room, being consoled by a couple of girls I knew, Ina and Wendy. She was mouthing off to them about the cheek of her (ex) boyfriend, and they were agreeing with her vehemently. She was obviously angry, too. Good.

"What the *hell* was the idea of that?" I asked, as I burst in. All three of them looked up, but it was pretty clear who I was talking to.

"The idea of what?" Helen replied.

"You got Stew riled up all the way, till he was about ready to go off, and then you come back and hide in *my house*? What were you thinking?"

"I didn't *hide*," she replied.

"Whatever you call it," I said, waving my hand to dismiss it. "Did you expect him to just turn around and walk away after you'd dumped him? Didn't you think he'd try and come after you?"

"I don't care what he does," she said, her voice rising in response to my own.

"Yeah, but I care, 'cause it's my house, and I could do without a fight in it," I shot back. That shut her up.

"Get off her back," said Ina, a short, pretty Asian girl that I used to fancy once-upon-a-time. I ignored her.

"You came without an invitation," I said to Helen. "That's okay, 'cause Cathy brought you. I don't mind that. But when you bring Stew along, then I do mind. I almost had a fight out there because of you. And you're the *last* person I'd consider worth fighting for." That was a particularly cutting piece of wit, I thought.

"What are you gonna do, kick me out?" said Helen, almost as if she was challenging me to do it.

"No," I said, without adding an explanation. I simply said: "Don't drag your boyfriend problems through my house."

"Jeez, you're uptight," she replied. Bitch.

"Eat shit," I said as my parting shot, and left.

She was right; I *was* uptight. But that's because it

44

was my first real party, and because it meant so much to me (for reasons I've already explained) and because, unlike a lot of people, I respect my parents a little and I didn't want to trash their house. I could bear the roasting I'd get when they got home, but I couldn't bear the disappointment in their eyes if they found out. And, in case you think I'd overreacted, let me tell you that Stew and Helen's fights were the stuff of legend. It just needed one person to touch off Stew inside my house and that was it – the end.

I'd averted disaster so far. But what I didn't know was that Stew wasn't finished with me yet.

Not by a long shot.

Chapter Five

When I returned downstairs to the party, I was feeling much better. I'd let off a bit of steam, and now I was okay. Still, I decided to sit out in the back garden for a bit in the cool night breeze. I was pretty sure there was somebody out there I could talk to, someone I could snag a beer off. I still had plenty of my own, but at the moment I couldn't be bothered to trek across my litter-strewn living room to get them. I also thought that Jo would be in there, and I wanted to chill out a bit, regain my composure, before I resumed my mission for the night.

Kerry Macclesfield was still in the kitchen, sitting on the breakfast counter. Her friends eyed me as I approached; I half-greeted them as I passed.

"That was pretty neat out there, Jay," said Kerry. I stopped and looked at her. She was being genuine. But I never have been all that good with compliments, and I didn't know what to say to it. I kind of mumbled "Cheers," I think. She gave me a strange smile then asked me if I had a light. I remembered my own cigarettes, and so I pulled one out of my packet and sparked us both up. Then I sauntered into the back garden, neatly stepping over the dopeheads on the doorstep.

The security light had turned on, activated by the motion of the people milling around outside, and the darkness of the night was held back by the furious glare. It was still a beautifully warm night, though, and I felt okay in just my T-shirt and baggies.

There were beer cans and bottles scattered all over the stone paving of the lower garden. I could see Thunderchunk in the distance, somewhere near the little grove at the back of my lawn, necking with his girlfriend in what they thought was the shadows. Closer by, sitting at one of the white plastic parasol tables, was Danny. I went over and sat next to him.

He pulled a Viborg out of his bag as soon as I sat down. I was about to protest – which was totally hypocritical, seeing as I was about to ask him for one – but he waved it off. "I owe you a few," he said. I couldn't remember if he did or not, so I took his word for it.

"What you up to, Danny?" I asked, conversationally.

"Not a lot," he replied. "I heard about what happened out front."

"Yeah, and where were *you*?" I said, prodding him playfully. "I could've got mauled out there."

Danny laughed. "Nah, you wouldn't need me. I'm a wuss."

"Where's Cathy?"

"Dunno," he replied, and from the tone of his voice I knew that something had gone on between them. Danny, however, didn't seem overly bothered by it.

I had never quite managed to fathom the attraction

that Danny and Cathy shared. The least little thing seemed to set them off on an argument. The smallest, pettiest things would have them at each other's throats. With anyone else, Danny had a patience and tolerance that was easily the equal of mine, but with her it was different. They seemed like arch-enemies who couldn't quite bring themselves to part, who enjoyed the conflict too much to split up. Neither of them ever had any kind of explanation for it, and Heaven knows I've wasted enough time thinking about it. Whatever it is that kept them together, it was something that they couldn't explain or put into words. Maybe the happiness they shared during the good times was precious enough to endure the frequent, savage squalls. Who could say? All I knew was, they had been going out together for over two years now, and I'd never had a relationship approaching that kind of length, so what did I know? And since when did rationality and reason ever come within missile range of romance? Not in my lifetime.

I had grown used to Danny and Cathy's turbulent relationship by now, and I knew that whatever had split them up this time, it was only temporary as always. Danny's good mood was undiminished, so he had either won the argument hands down or he knew as well as me that they'd be back together within a few hours.

"Something's up with Cappo," I said, changing tack.

"No kidding," Danny replied. "He's hardly spoken all night."

"How do you know?" I asked, amused. "You haven't been near him since Cathy arrived."

"Sam mentioned it a while ago," he explained.

I chuffed on my B&H. "Yeah, well, I'm a bit worried. I mean, we all have our moods once in a while, but Cappo . . . he sort of coasts on top of it all, doesn't he? He doesn't get down about stuff. Not usually."

"He'll talk to us when he's ready," Danny said.

"Perhaps I should go and see him," I mused, rubbing the back of my neck and coming dangerously close to igniting my hair with the tip of my cigarette.

"You want to concentrate on that Jo girl," said Danny, giving me a conspiratorial wink. "You seemed to be doing alright before."

I grinned. "You reckon?"

Danny rocked back on his chair, his beer sloshing over the edge of his can. "You were doing just fine. If I were you, I'd get back in there."

"After these," I said, meaning my drink and my cigarette.

"Playing it laid-back, huh?" said Danny, smirking. "I like it."

Danny's ribbing was just getting me embarrassed, so I changed the subject. "What do you think are the chances of Sam getting blasted enough to try it on with Kerry Macclesfield?" I asked mischievously.

Danny cackled. "Again? No way. He'd have to be absolutely melted to try again, after we destroyed him last time."

I raised an eyebrow, James Bond style. "Lay money on that?"

"I haven't got any," said Danny.

"Let's make it a gentleman's bet, then. I say Sam's going to try it on with Kerry."

"Okay, if you say so," said Danny, shaking my hand.

I didn't really think that Sam was going to go for it; I was just messing around. We had a laugh while we finished our beers, and I thought how lucky I was to have friends as cool as this.

I found Jo again soon after. I bumped into Sam as he was getting a beer from the fridge (someone else's) and he said that she was in the lounge. I made my way there and sat down next to her; she looked pleased to see me, and a radiant smile lit up her features. She could turn me to a quivering mush with that smile. I wondered if she was aware of that.

I found another can and offered it to her. She had finished her bottle of wine now, and I imagined that she was probably pretty axed; she didn't show it though, just stayed classy and bright. Not like Stew.

She accepted my gift, and we clinked cans before drinking.

"So where'd you go, stranger?" she said.

"Here and there," I replied. "I was a bit wound up about Stew."

"I thought you handled it really well," she said.

I blushed, I think. She laughed lightly at my evident embarrassment.

"Ah, come on. Don't be bashful."

Someone jostled by me, shifting position nearby. I looked for Cappo and saw that he wasn't around. The room was getting suffocatingly hot, even though the windows were open. Someone had switched my Orbital CD for a Future Sound Of London album.

"Do you want to go someplace else?" I said, on impulse.

Jo nodded, her eyes fixed on mine in a way that I liked. I loved the clean lines of her eyes, the almost oriental curve of her eyelids. I felt a hot flush of desire, sudden and overwhelming; but I had to fight it back, keep it cool, while I led the way out of the lounge, through the pockets of people lolling about on the lime-green carpet.

I was sure that I was swaying as I crossed the room. I certainly didn't feel steady on my feet. When I looked back at Jo, she seemed to be moving as lithely as a cat in comparison, but that could have been just because our swaying was in sync. Who knows?

We made our way out into the hallway, and up the stairs, and Jo selected a spot on the upstairs landing. She leaned her back against the wall and then slid down it to sit, cross-legged. I sat down next to her, my legs making a bridge across the landing, my heels resting on the banister supports. I was well relaxed.

"This your first party?" she asked.

"Yeah. Well, you know, the first one that I've *organized*. Not the first one I've been to."

"You did alright, I reckon," she said.

"Ah, well," I replied neutrally. "I didn't really do anything. I suppose these things go by themselves. I'm not much of a host. I haven't talked to half of the people here yet."

"That's 'cause I've been taking up your time," she said playfully.

Astute girl, I thought. I wonder if she's guessed yet? How I feel about her, I mean?

"Yeah," I said, trying to think of the least mawkish thing to say. "Still, it was time well spent." Hoboy, was *that* a bad line. I cursed my paralyzed mental abilities.

"I liked how you handled Stew," she said. "I thought you looked really brave out there."

"I didn't feel brave," I admitted, shrugging slightly.

Jo laughed. "I know. Stew's quite a bit bigger than you."

"I suppose I'd set my mind on having a really decent party," I explained. "Remember Dod's party... Oh, you didn't go, did you?"

She shook her head.

"Well, he just invited anyone, said everybody could come along. Course, when you've got strangers in your house, they don't give a damn what they do. His house looked like the Zone after they'd finished with it."

"Slack," she commented.

"I just didn't want Stew in my house. He's a dickhead," I finished simply.

We shared a few moments of comfortable silence.

She took a drink from her can. "It's been..." she began, then she kind of tailed off.

"What?" I prompted. "It's been what?"

"It's been good talking to you tonight," she said, her eyes fixed on her knees in what I supposed was embarrassment. *Her* embarrassed? "Really talking, I mean. Obviously we're both a bit drunk and all, I know that, but ... I don't know. I kind of think that I never really got to know you in our English classes." She looked at me. "I wish I'd done this sooner."

"Same here," I said, in deadly earnest. Almost before I could stop it, my hand slipped into hers. I braced myself for the squeal of rejection that I knew must come ... but nothing happened. She kept my hand in hers, stroking the back of it with her thumb.

I looked up into her heart-shaped face, framed by that golden bob, with those gloriously exotic eyes, and she was looking back at me, filling me with electric excitement. And all at once I knew that, whatever happened tonight, I really wanted to see this girl again, *really*, not just a one-night thing but the whole whack. And the sudden realization of that, and the way she was gazing at me, made me a little giddy.

"Jay! I need to talk to you!"

No! It was Cathy, standing in the bathroom doorway, tears streaking her face, making her nose and cheeks a wet red.

I came this close to telling her to sod off. Her sense of timing was cruel. But I couldn't. And, anyway, it was too late. Jo had perceived that Cathy was in distress, and was evidently expecting me to attend to her.

I got up sourly, levering myself into a standing position, reluctantly relinquishing my hold on Jo's hand. I gave her a kind of apologetic glance, but she smiled warmly and said, "Don't worry, I'm not going anywhere." It was as if she'd read my mind. Well, to be honest, it wasn't that much of a feat; my face tends to show whatever emotion I'm feeling at the time. With Cathy, I was making a gargantuan effort not to show her how irritated I was.

I went into the bathroom with Cathy. She closed and locked the door behind me. My bathroom is pretty big, I suppose. It's got a huge tub, all white and smooth, with gold-effect taps. Or it could be brass, I don't know. Shiny, anyway. The toilet seat and tank are made of polished wood, and there are light brown tasselled bathrugs strewn over the cream-coloured carpet. The whole place has a warm, cosy ambience – unusual for a bathroom, I think. But at that moment my mind wasn't on the decor of the bathroom; I was hoping that Cathy had a really, *really* good reason for calling me in to talk to her.

I couldn't stay irked for long, though. I mean, she was in tears right in front of me. I knew that Cathy sometimes started crying for the most silly reasons, but I couldn't help softening. "What's up, Cath?" I said.

She sat down on the varnished wood toilet seat. I perched on the lip of the bath nearby. I still had my can of beer welded to my hand, and I took a swig while I waited for Cathy to respond. She wasn't really *crying*, like when you're sobbing great big whoops of air; I suppose you'd call it weeping.

"Oh, you don't want to know," she sniffed wetly.

"Then why did you call me in here?" I said, a little heartlessly.

The logic of that defeated her. "It's Danny," she confessed. What – a – *surprise*!

"What about him?" I asked cautiously.

She wrinkled her cute, freckled nose and bowed her head so her coppery hair spilled forward over her face. "We had a fight," she said.

"Yeah, I guessed as much," I replied. "Hey, it's nothing to get upset about." I patted her on the shoulder in what I hoped was a comforting fashion.

"Over you," she said.

"What?" I was dumbfounded. My hand froze in mid-pat.

"The fight was over you," she repeated.

The words OH SHIT paraded through my head in huge alabaster letters.

"Why over me?" I asked, praying that it wasn't what I thought it was.

Cathy brushed her hair back behind her ear. "I told him that I fancied you," she said, like she was pronouncing a death sentence.

I stood up explosively. "You *what*? Why?"

"Only a little bit!" she protested. "Not as much as him!"

I bit off the reply I was going to make to that, modified it a little before replying. "Of all the dumb things in the world to tell your boyfriend, that takes the damn biscuit! *Why?*"

"Because it's the truth," she sobbed.

I was really sick of her now. "But what was the point in telling him? How could you be so *stupid*?"

I remembered the conversation I'd had with Danny

out in the back garden, how he'd been reluctant to elaborate on the reasons for their fight. He'd seemed alright about it then, but now I thought: maybe he was just putting on a front? Maybe he was really pissed off at me? Why couldn't my life just be simple for a few minutes?

Suddenly she was holding on to me, with her arms around my waist, her body pressed to mine. "But I meant it," she was saying, about an inch from my lips, and I was drunk, and it would have been so *easy* to kiss her then, but it would have been so *wrong*.

I shoved her off me. "Get lost, Cathy," I said cruelly. She looked at me with a wounded expression in her eyes. "Now get this straight: you are my best friend's girlfriend, and you can*not* act like this. Can't you be responsible for a second? Didn't you think what it might do to me and Danny as friends when you told him that you fancied me?"

She was just gazing blankly at me.

"You can't understand, can you? I don't think you even know what you're *doing* half the time!"

"Jay..." she started to protest, but I wasn't listening. I knew if I stayed, I'd say something I really didn't want to, and while Cathy was a girl with huge psychological problems, she was still my friend. So I left, tearing open the lock and slamming the bathroom door behind me.

Jo was looking at me with concern etched in her face. "What's wrong, Jay?" she asked.

I was about to reply when a shout went up from the back garden. Not just a shout, more a battle-cry.

"What now?" I groaned, then glanced at Jo. "I'll have to tell you later," I said, then thundered down the stairs to find out what the commotion was.

Chapter Six

"What's going on?" I asked as I plunged into the milling throng of people in my back garden. The night had turned colder, and the blazing glare of the security light mercilessly illuminated every feature on every face.

It was Pete who answered me. "It's Stew. He's back, and he's brought some friends." He looked a bit scared.

"Then what's everyone doing in my back garden?" I asked.

"They've come over the fields," said Pete anxiously. "From the Zone."

I mumbled an epithet and made my way forward. There was another group of people, mainly boys, gathered around the copse of trees at the end of my garden. I sprinted the grassy expanse in between and joined them.

Inside the copse, shadowy faces moved carefully, like commandos staking out a target. The security light didn't reach this far down the garden; there was only the ambient glow of the night to see by, and much of that was blocked by the branches of the trees. I wove through to the front, where I could get a decent view of what was going on, and found myself standing next to Rich, the Thunderchunk.

"Alright, Jay," he said, his eyes narrowed and looking ahead. I followed his gaze. Approaching across the fields were four – no, five – figures. It was too dark, and they were too far away to see who they were. Has Stew brought some of the zombies from the Square? I thought with a momentary burst of fear. No, Stew didn't have the kind of whack to get those guys away from their plastic bags and needles.

"Who shouted a minute ago?" I said, settling next to Rich.

He smirked. I could sense it in the tone of his voice rather than see it. "That was me," he said. "Pretty good, huh? I saw 'em coming from here. I had to give the alarm."

"And what were you *doing* way back here in the trees?" I asked slyly, remembering his girlfriend. Rich harrumphed exaggeratedly, feigning embarrassment, and we both laughed. It was strange. I mean, the whole thing was kind of scary, but was it ever *exciting*! It was like High Noon, with those five varmints tracking over the fields towards us, obviously intending to cause trouble. And then there was a whole group of us, watching and observing from our screen of trees, like we were ready to spring an ambush (even though, after Rich's shout, they must have known where we were). It reminded me of a time when I'd been on one of those paintball wargames with Sam; the mingled excitement and fear was a heady concoction.

We outnumbered them, I reckoned, doing a quick

count of who was hiding in or around the copse. I didn't count the ones who hung back, like Pete; they wouldn't be any help. Problem was, Stew and the crew from class 11B were used to fights and rumbles; at least, more so than our guys. I didn't know who would fold and run if it came to a fight.

"Where's the others?" I asked Rich.

"Danny's over the other side somewhere. I haven't seen Sam or Cappo."

I was a little disappointed. I had hoped that they'd be here. As for Danny, well ... at that moment, with Cathy's confession fresh in my mind (*why* did she do it?), I didn't have the guts to go up and face him. I know it wasn't my fault and all, but I still felt funny about it. And right now, I had other, more urgent problems.

"Jay!" called one of the shadowy figures. They were still a way away, but it was a clear night and his voice carried well. Everybody hushed. It was Stew.

"I'm here," I called back.

"Come over here so I can talk to you," came the slurred bellow.

I laughed derisively. "How stupid do you think I am?" I called back. "Five of you and one of me? Yeah, right. Nice try." I was still feeling pretty belligerent, with all the beer in my system. Still, I told myself not to be so flip. Even when he was plastered, Stew was an enemy I wouldn't wish on anyone.

"We won't hurt'cha."

"Course you won't, Stew," I said sarcastically. Then I went a little more serious. "Don't you reckon all this is going a bit far just to get Helen to come to your party? Can't you just see her tomorrow?"

"This isn't about Helen any more," Stew cried. "She can spin for all I care."

Uh-oh.

"Then what are you here for?" I shouted.

"We're here for *you*," came the reply. I knew it. I'd pushed him, and he wanted revenge.

In the copse with me, everyone was silent, expectant, waiting to see what I would do. I smiled invisibly to myself. I was the General. My army against his army. Those prepared to defend my party (or who were pissed up and lairy and willing to have a fight) against Stew and his boys. Truth be told, most of the guys on my side didn't much like the 11B crew anyway, and with school now over, this was a God-given opportunity to get back at them for years of irritating swagger and intimidation.

The silence stretched out, the anticipation building unbearably.

"Come and get me, then," I said, and everyone in the copse cheered noisily. Boy, they were spoiling for it alright. A fierce grin spread across my face. I couldn't help it.

I think it was the sound of the cheers that made Stew and his guys falter. They hadn't been able to see how many were hiding in the trees that separated my garden from the fields; the volume of the response dismayed them. Probably it sounded like more, but I reckoned we outnumbered them two to one. Ten of us to five of them.

"Don't go out to them," I whispered to Rich, next to me. "Let them come in here. It's so dark, nobody'll know what's going on."

"That's letting them get awfully close to your house," Rich replied doubtfully, shifting his wide bulk in the darkness with a rustle of grass. "Why let them get that near? We can take 'em out there if they get any closer. There's more of us."

"Yeah, but if we make a charge, how many people can you guarantee will come with us?"

"You, me; Poddy'll definitely come, he hates Stew; Macca; Ben... What about Danny?"

"I couldn't say. I've never seen him in a fight before," I replied.

"Five, then," said Rich.

I scratched the back of my neck, watching the slow approach of Stew and his men. "That's not good enough. Macca's a psycho, but he's only small. Poddy's a beanpole. I'm not much of a combat veteran myself. We need numbers."

I was discussing tactics with my second-in-command. How cool was that?

Stew and his gang stopped, ten metres or so away in the darkness. "Come on, then," one of the faceless figures demanded.

"Come in and get us," I replied quickly, before anybody rose to the challenge.

"What's up? Chicken?"

I sighed to myself. *So* original. Of course, the only

thing worse than someone who used a line like that was somebody who *fell* for it. And, unfortunately, Poddy was just that stupid.

"I ain't scared of a pack of retards like you," he said, as he stepped out of the copse on to the open ground.

"Damn," I said to myself. We'd just forfeited our best advantage: cover. Now that Poddy had shown himself, he couldn't very well retreat into hiding again. He'd lose too much face. And we couldn't leave him out there on his own.

Nobody needed telling; everyone stepped forward on to the battlefield.

I looked at our side. Seven of us had assembled on the grass, the trees at our backs; three had wimped out. I caught Danny's eye in the darkness – he was one of the seven – but I couldn't see his expression. Then he looked away, to concentrate on the danger. So did I.

Now there are fights, and there are fights. School fights involved a bit of a punch up, mostly body-blows, the odd jaw-hit once in a while. Really, school fights are about pride; you want to get enough decent hits in before the teacher comes to break it up, but you don't really want to damage your opponent.

Street fights, on the other hand, are another league of viciousness. I cringed when I thought of some of the stuff I'd seen in town on a Friday night. Head-butts, rib-kicks on a guy when he's down, elbows, knees, boots; street fights are usually won by the other guy being put in hospital.

I wondered distantly as we faced each other; was this to be a school fight or a street fight? All my side were school fighters. We didn't possess the ability to beat somebody severely; we wouldn't be able to bring ourselves to do it. Well, maybe Macca could, but he was too small to do anyone any lasting damage.

But I wasn't sure about the other side. Sure, at school they were all strut and swagger, but I knew that some of them – especially Stew – had been in some proper scrapes before. A school fight hurt, but a street fight was *dangerous*. If these guys were nasty enough, something really bad might happen to us. I tried not to think about it, only about the things I was defending: my house, my pride, and myself.

We were at some sort of impasse. Facing off, nobody knew quite what to do. Were we going to fight, or were we just going to exchange insults? It needed a spark to set it off. Taking advantage of the pause, I thought that maybe I could defuse the situation.

"Stew," I said. "Listen, there's no point to this. I'm just trying to have a party, and so are you." I sounded like a coward, but I didn't care. I didn't want to fight him.

"Shoulda thought of that before you started on me," Stew replied. "Now you get what's coming to you."

"You made me do that, Stew. You know you did," I replied reasonably. "If this is anyone's fault, it's Helen's. Take it up with her."

Stew swayed a bit. I could only really see his outline, him and his shadowy colleagues. He seemed to consider what I had said. That, at least, was encouraging. His response was not.

"No," he said finally. "You started a fight, and then you got your mate to back you up. Well now *my* mates are here, and we can settle this."

"We can settle it without having a scrap," I protested. Yeah, I really did sound like a wuss. I thought for a moment that I might have got through to him. I guess I'll never know, because right then somebody behind me – presumably Macca – shouted: "Cut the shit and let's fight!"

The spark was thrown.

Both sides rushed forward, me and Stew heading for each other. I was conscious only of frantic movement all around; it was so dark, and we were all drunk, and I don't think anyone really knew what was going on. When we clashed, the fists seemed to fly faster that the eye could take them in. It was chaotically confusing.

Stew landed me a good one in the stomach; I didn't even see it, but I felt it alright. I think it should have winded me, but for some reason it didn't. Stew was surprised about that, because I came back fast, swinging a punch at his jaw, going more by instinct than sight. There was a satisfying jolt of impact up my arm, and I thought: That's it, I've won.

But it's not like in the movies; any idiot knows that. His eyes didn't roll up into his head and he didn't collapse to the floor, KO'd by a clean hit to the jaw.

No, he just got madder. In fact, he went pretty well apeshit on me.

I faltered under the flailing flurry of blows that he threw at me. His teeth were bared in a snarl of anger, and his eyes glittered viciously. Somehow I grabbed his arm as he flashed a fist at my nose; he thundered into me, and we both went down hard on the grass.

I was aware of the thud and smack of fists around me, the grunts of the other combatants; but me and Stew were in a private little combat of our own, ignored by the others, the two Generals locked in battle. He thrashed his way on top of me, trying to hold my arms down so he could get a punch in at my unprotected face. Frantically trying to evade his grasping hands, I drove a knee hard into his kidneys from behind. He grunted in pain and straightened, freeing my arms; I took the opportunity to lay another one on his jaw before he rolled off me. We both sprang to our feet, facing each other.

His hand went to his cheek, which must have been giving him some pain even in his drunken state. "You're dead," he said flatly.

"Don't reckon so," I replied with a breathless grin. His coordination was all off due to the amount of whisky he had drunk. I was wasted, yeah, but I wasn't as bad as he was by a long chalk. After that first scuffle, I began to think: Hey, I can win this!

He flew at me again, and this time I sidestepped and tripped him. It was hilarious. He went sprawling across the grass, face down. I could have pressed the advantage, but I'm not much into kicking people when they're down. He got back to his feet, and though I couldn't see it, I knew his face must have been purple with rage.

Then we really went at it; punches flew between us, with no thought for precision or dodging. There was no circling each other and jabbing swiftly to foil the opponent's guard. We just tried to batter each other. The blows weren't very hard by either of us, but they were enough to hurt. I got a nasty crack on my left cheek and a dead arm, but Stew came off worse. See, his blows were even wilder than mine, because he was drunk and angry. After one particularly bad overswing, I got three hits in to his face. *Bam-bam-bam*. And that was it.

He stumbled backwards, tripped over his feet and landed on his butt, glaring at me. I thought he was going to come at me again as he got to his feet, so I made myself ready. But he didn't. Instead he spat on the ground in front of me, and turned away with a look of disgust on his face. Presumably that was his way of saying that I wasn't worth fighting. Or it could've been because he'd had enough and wanted to bow out with as much pride as he could salvage. Either way, he was done.

"Leave it," he shouted to his crew. They stopped and backed off. We'd fought them to a standstill. Both sides were bruised, some were bloodied, but nobody on my side had given up.

Stew faced me across the newly-drawn lines of our troops. "I'm not gonna forget this," he growled at me. Then, to his friends: "Come on. We'll leave 'em to their gay little party."

"Assholes," someone on my side muttered. Macca again, I reckon. One of theirs went lunging back towards him, ready to restart the fight, but he was dragged back and calmed by his friends. Macca didn't push it any further, thankfully.

We didn't move as we watched them go. My hands throbbed dully, and my body too, but I was hardly aware of the pain. I could barely believe what was happening. We had repelled the invaders. We were victorious! I felt suddenly elated. My legs were beginning to shake a little from all the excitement. I thought that I should say something to my troops (yeah, I was really getting into the idea of being a General now), but all I could think of was: "Thanks, guys. I owe you one."

Rich stood at my shoulder. "No problem," he said. "It was fun, right?" This last was addressed to everyone else, who responded with murmurings of assent.

The group began to break up and filter back to the party. I looked for Danny, but he had been one of the first to leave. I had to have a talk with him, I decided. Sort things out. But for the moment, standing in the clear night on an open field, with Rich next to me, I basked in the moment of victory and felt brilliant.

Chapter Seven

I returned to the party a few minutes later. From the end of my garden, as I approached, my house looked great. Brightly lit upstairs windows cut holes in the dark brick, and the panoramic flood of the security light cast long shadows across the paving slabs of the lower garden. The whole place was a hive of activity; if you strained, it was possible to hear the music coming from the lounge. This was *my* party, I thought with pride, and it was going well.

Actually, that was oversimplifying things. It wasn't going all that well for me. I knew that the bruises Stew had dealt me – mainly on my body – were going to kill in the morning. And I still had no idea what on earth possessed Cathy to tell Danny that she fancied me. I mean, it probably wasn't even *true*; at least I didn't think so. I don't know; it would take a legion of trained psychiatrists to know what went on inside that girl's mind. But it irked me that she might have jeopardized mine and Danny's friendship.

On the other hand, there was Jo, and I was pretty darn pleased with how things seemed to be going with her. Now if I could get some peace for five minutes, I might be able to resume what we had started. I was a little paranoid about stuff like that; I had this horrible feeling that she'd be snatched away from me while I wasn't there, or that she'd go home or something. I decided to make that my priority; I had to go and find her.

Just five minutes of peace. Alas, it was not to be.

I wandered back through the kitchen, where I noticed that Kerry Macclesfield was surprisingly absent. All that was left were a few bottles of Castaway on the breakfast bar. I wonder if she'd managed to pull. A smile tugged at my face at the thought.

I made a bit of headway, acknowledging greetings but not stopping to chat. I wanted to find Jo, and I didn't want to get sidetracked again. Already, I could picture the smoothness of her cheeks, the curve of her eyelids. Eager with anticipation, I went upstairs, to where she had promised to wait for me.

But she wasn't there. Cappo was. And he looked in a right state. He hazily registered me as I came into view. In his hand was a bottle of some kind of cheap spirit. He looked white, like he was really sick. Suddenly concerned, I sat down next to him. With a terrible stab of guilt, I realized that I'd practically ignored him all night, because he'd been in such a bad mood. Some friend I was. I'd been chasing after a girl instead. I felt really slack.

"Are you alright, Cappo?" I asked. He didn't answer. "Neil? You alright?"

He tried to take another swig from his bottle, but I could see that he'd had too much already. I gently prised it out of his hands. "Come on, man, enough of that," I said.

"Gimme me bottle back," he spat. But he just lay there like a limp jellyfish, too melted to do anything about it.

"How much have you drunk tonight?" I asked.

There was a pause before he answered, during which his head kind of lolled to one side. "Not enough," he replied.

"Is that what you've been doing? Drinking on your own? I saw how much alcohol you had in that bag."

"So what?" he mumbled. "I can drink on me own if I want. Don't need no ... don't need anybody else."

I felt awful. He'd been laying alcohol down himself all night and nobody had been with him. There was something terribly wrong. I'd suspected it when I first saw him tonight, but I just let it go. What a jerk I was! I really hated myself at that moment, for being so callous. Nobody had ever actually got round to asking him what was up.

Well, I was going to sort that out right now. Forget Jo, forget Danny, at the moment Cappo had a real problem, and I was damned if I was going to desert him until he was straightened out.

"What is it?" I asked. "You never drink like this. You're drinking to forget, aren't you? What's happened?"

"Nothing's happened," he said.

"Come off it, Cappo. It's obvious. You've been depressed all night," I shook his shoulder in a matey sort of way, "and we know you're always the bouncy one among us. It's gotta be something pretty bad to bring you low. So spill: what is it?"

Cappo looked at me despairingly. Then he suddenly scrambled to his feet and blundered into the bathroom. I followed him in, and saw him drop to his knees in front of the toilet. He just managed to raise the seat before he chucked up his guts with a disgustingly ripe splashing sound. I closed the door of the bathroom behind me and locked it.

Cappo was sick, and sick, and *sick*. I was thinking of calling an ambulance at one point. It just seemed like he was never going to stop. It was like he was purging his entire body in one go. Every time he managed to stop long enough to catch his breath, I thought that he had finished; and then he'd do some of those horrible gassy retch-burps and the chunder would plunge out of him again. If it had been anyone else, it would have been side-splitting. But I was too worried about him to laugh.

He hung his head over the toilet basin for a while, breathing heavily, his face red and sweaty. After a few moments, he shakily reached up a hand and flushed the toilet, then replaced the seat and kind of slumped to the ground. But he was okay, though. From where I was sitting – on the edge of the bath – I could see he felt better.

I asked him anyway. "You alright now?"

"Muuuch better," he groaned. I couldn't tell if he was being sarcastic or not.

"Wanna talk?" I said.

"Don't you give up?" he replied, his voice slurred because his cheek was pressed to the carpet of the toilet floor.

"Nope," I answered.

He took a great big sigh. I saw his back rise and fall. Then he told me.

"My parents are splitting up."

I didn't know what to say. So I said something stupid. It happens to me a lot. "You sure?"

Cappo sort of smiled bitterly. "No, it's just a vicious rumour," he replied. This time he *was* being sarcastic.

"Sorry, that was a dumb thing to say."

"S'alright."

"How long have you known?"

"Since today," said Cappo. "They told me just before I came round here. I didn't want to be in the house with them."

I remembered Cappo's moodiness with his dad when he had been dropped off at my house. It all made sense now.

"You know what, though?" he went on. "They were gonna do it for ages. They agreed a long while ago. But they didn't tell me."

"Why not?"

"Because..." he began, but then his voice wavered and his eyes began to fill with tears. "Because they said they didn't want to interfere with my *concentration* for the exams." That was it; he really began bawling. I didn't know what to do. There's something awful about seeing one of your close friends cry. I mean, maybe it's alright for girls, I wouldn't know. But for boys, well; you've got to be *really* messed up to cry in front of one of your mates.

I slid down on to the floor next to him and sort of put my arm around his shoulders. It was awkward, with how he was lying, crumpled and face-down, but I managed. It felt strange, I was almost embarrassed about doing it, but afterwards it felt sort of comforting. To me, that is. I hope it did the same for him.

"I mean," he sobbed. "Doesn't that just beat it all? They didn't tell me they were getting a divorce 'cause of a few crappy exams. They had fights and stuff, but I didn't think it was anything major. I didn't even *know*."

I squeezed his shoulder sympathetically.

"I'm old enough to understand what it's about and all," Cappo continued. "Divorce and stuff. But you never think it's going to happen to your parents. I mean, you don't even appreciate them until you realize that they're not gonna *be* there any more." He sniffed loudly, a tear running down his nose. "Everything that was stable has suddenly gone," he said. "It's like, the first time you ever realize the *world* is out there, and one day you're gonna have to face it on your own."

I didn't really understand what he was saying. How could I? I was lucky enough to have parents who still seemed to be in love. If it had been anyone's parents, I would say that it would be Sam's folks who'd have split up, with all the arguing they do. But Cappo's?

I just sat there, feeling awkward, while Cappo told me everything. He told me all the fears and the questions that his parents' announcement had raised in him. It was like he was trying to sort them out in his own head by telling someone else. I listened, and I tried to understand, and I felt sorry for him. And I realized once more that we had all been a little selfish tonight – me, Danny and Sam – because we hadn't made the time to find out what was wrong. I really began to feel bad about it. Really.

I remembered how he'd reacted when we'd been talking about the subject of boys and girls getting along, and I remembered how bitter he'd been. I should have at least had an inkling then. But no, my thoughts were on Jo, and I let it slip by. What an idiot I was.

So we sat there for a bit, and we talked. I got him some water from the sink, tried to dilute some of the alcohol out of his body (yeah, like *that* was gonna work), and I stayed with him. It had been a terrible blow for him, I could see that. So I stuck by him while he tried to come to terms with it, and I tried to be as supportive as I could.

In the end, however, he'd talked himself out. I told him that it wouldn't be as bad as it first appeared – nothing ever is – and he seemed to calm down a bit, and he stopped crying. I mean, what I was saying wasn't doing any good, I don't reckon; I just think he needed to tell someone, and that someone was me.

"I'm sorry, Jay," he said eventually.

"What for?"

"You know, dumping all this on you and stuff."

"Don't be stupid," I said. "I wish you'd told me earlier, before you got battered."

"I just knew I'd start crying if I told anyone," he

replied. He had got up from the floor by now, and was sitting on the toilet with the lid down. I was back on the edge of the bath. A couple of people had banged on the bathroom door, wanting to be let in, but I told them to go to the downstairs loo. Presumably they thought I was getting it on in here or something; anyway, they left us alone.

"You're not often wrong," I said, grinning. He sniffed and laughed quietly. It was good to hear him laugh.

"Guess not," he said. Then he kind of sighed. "Ah, you'd better go now. I'm okay. You've got a party to see to. And there's Jo, isn't there?"

I felt a little embarrassed that my attentions had been so transparently obvious. "What about her?" I said.

Cappo laughed again. "Come on, Jay. You're *gagging* for it."

I blushed. "Maybe," I replied.

"Get out there, then."

"You sure you're okay?"

"Yeah. Thanks for being here."

Those words made it all seem worthwhile. "No problem," I said. Of all of us, it was Cappo that was going to be staying on at school with me next year. I felt happy that at least I wasn't going to lose *him*.

"See you," he said, and I left him.

As I was making my way back down the stairs, slipping by a snogging couple who had chosen to perch halfway up (how awkward can you get?), it suddenly occurred to me that I still didn't know where Jo was. It may sound like an easy task to find somebody at a house party, but experience told me that this was very rarely the case. People wandered off to 24-hour shops, they disappeared into secluded corners with their chosen partner for the night, they went to explore the attic and fell asleep there, and so on. Also, there are potential no-go zones at house parties, where you have to be very careful about who you barge in on. Yes, even in my own house, I was well aware that there were some rooms you just didn't go into. The bedrooms, mostly.

I was feeling a little better about myself now. In the end, I'd been there for Cappo, and it was better late than never. He'd taken the first step towards dealing with his parents' divorce; but we both knew that it would take a whole lot more than that to sort out his messed-up head. I fully intended to go back and see him, but I was aware that the night was drawing on, and I really wanted to find Jo and sort stuff out with her. Then I'd have to see Danny. Oh, why was everything so complicated?

I'd reached the bottom of the stairs before I realized that the wriggling couple on the steps was actually Kerry Macclesfield and Pete. Who'd have thought it? I smiled to myself and left them alone. Pete's hardly a babe-magnet at the best of times but, well, Kerry had a quota to fill. People still remembered with fondness that legendary party in March when she *didn't* manage to pull somebody. I tell you, it must be way easier for girls than boys; pissed-up boys will go for anything with a pulse, whereas girls can afford to be choosy. Still I was a little put out that I'd lost my bet with Danny. I supposed that Sam wasn't going to pull Kerry tonight; Pete had got there first. Still, you never know...

I went through the lounge this time, looking for Jo. I didn't want to ask anybody if they'd seen her; that would give the game away. Instead, I scanned the groups of people clustered around my furniture.

The party had thinned out noticably in here, as people drifted away to fall into a drunken coma, get it on with their partner of choice; or go home and go to bed (those who lived close enough). However, there were still quite a few sticking around, having a laugh. I didn't spot Jo among them, but my head was pretty fuzzy and my vision didn't seem to move as fast as my head did. I'd sort of turn my head to the left and the pictures would lazily amble along afterwards, taking their time to settle in front of my eyes.

I looked closer, afraid that I'd miss her. But she wasn't there.

Undeterred, I poked into the kitchen – which was empty, surprisingly; I guess it was no fun there without Kerry – and then out into the back garden. The upper garden was full of people, who had all sat down in a rough circle in the grass and were playing some kind of game that involved a lot of good-natured screaming and laughing. I vaguely hoped that my vampire neighbours wouldn't complain at all the noise this late at night, but I really didn't care too much at this point.

I looked around the back a bit, but I couldn't see Jo anywhere. It was beginning to worry me now; where had she gone? She'd said that she wasn't going anywhere, when I'd gone to talk with Cathy. Had she gone home while I was out slugging with Stew (I felt my ribs begin to throb at the memory)? Had I missed my only chance?

No, I wouldn't accept that. I knew that she had to be here somewhere, and I was going to find her.

I scanned around the people who were sitting in my back garden, but I came up blank again. She wasn't out here. That left only two places I hadn't checked: the front garden and the upstairs bedrooms.

A quick glance out of my front door put paid to the first possibility. There was nobody out there but a couple necking by the hedge. The girl had a different hairstyle to Jo, so I knew it wasn't her. But the sight sparked in me a sudden thought. Like I say, sometimes I'm quite a paranoid person, and I got to thinking that maybe Jo was with someone else at the moment. You know what I mean.

I started imagining these scenes as I turned away and went up the stairs. I pictured Jo sitting alone on the landing while I was out in the back garden, sorting out Stew. One of the guys at the party comes up to her, starts talking to her 'cause she's alone, one thing leads to another and... I don't know, maybe I have a shameful lack of faith in other human beings, but I was working myself up into a right state about it. Maybe I'd missed my chance, because I'd gone to deal with Cathy's hysteria. Maybe Jo had gone off with someone else.

I reached the top of the stairs just as the door to my bedroom was opening. It almost seemed to happen in slow-motion. I heard Jo's laugh from that doorway, and the sound made my heart sink. Because I knew she was laughing with someone. And as she emerged from the doorway – the doorway to my *bedroom*, the first choice place for a bit of snogging at a party – I saw someone coming out with her. I felt suddenly cold all over as I saw who it was. Sam, my friend Sam, ladykiller Sam, with the girl that I fancied more than anybody else in the world.

I knew what they'd been doing in there. I had to duck away, back down the stairs, before they saw me. If I had to talk to Sam at that moment, I think I would've said something that I would've regretted. Because I hated him right then. I really hated him.

Chapter Eight

Someone shouted "Midnight!" in the lounge, and for some reason the whole room cheered. I didn't know what they were up to in there; I didn't care. I was sitting on the wall in my front garden (the necking couple had gone by now), smoking a cigarette and tapping my heels on the brick while I scowled at the pavement. It occurred to me that I was back where I started, four or five hours ago, when I first saw Danny coming down the road in a halo of sunlight. Except now it was night, and everything seemed to have gone wrong.

How *could* he? That was all I could think of. How could Sam *do* that to me? I mean, it's been an unwritten law since the beginning of time: you don't try and pull the girl your mate fancies. And you sure as hell don't *succeed*! If I'd have known I was in the running against Sam, I would have given up long ago. But I had no idea that he fancied her.

And that was the worst of it. Sam probably *didn't* fancy her much. I'd seen it happen before. He'd got off with Jo for no more reason than to pass the time, and then forget about her tomorrow. She'd burn her friends' ears about it for ages, going on about what an ignorant sod he was, and eventually it'd all be forgotten. Except by me, who'd had my only chance at going out with Jo torn away from me by one of my best friends. Lord, it was so *unfair*.

Yeah, that's right. I was whining self-piteously to myself while I was sitting on that wall, chuffing on my Benson. Everyone's entitled to a bit of self-pity now and again; I was cramming a whole year's worth into one night. I was gutted by what Sam had done, by what *Jo* had done. And I felt bad, really bad. Suddenly, more than anything else, I wanted to see Stew again, so I could really take it out on him. But I knew I'd have no such luck.

How could Jo do it? We'd been sitting in that corridor, on the verge of . . . *something*, when Cathy had stuck her oar in and messed everything up. Jo had said then: "Don't worry, I'm not going anywhere." Or something along those lines. Then, while I was outside, she went and got off with Sam! She was fast, I'll give her that. The whole thing left me bitter.

I must have been out there for a while before I heard the front door open behind me. I heard footsteps approaching across the small front lawn, and then I heard a voice from over my shoulder.

"There you are. I've been looking all over the place for you."

It was Jo.

"I'll bet you have," I replied under my breath.

She sat down next to me. In the wash of light from the streetlamps, she looked just as pretty as ever. I hated her, with the kind of unreasoning passion that only a wronged lover can feel. (Did I say *lover*? Oops.)

"I heard about what happened out back. Are you hurt?"

"I'm okay," I replied curtly, sounding all the wounded martyr.

"I thought you were going to come back and see me when it was all over," she continued, oblivious to the tone of my voice.

"You weren't there," I replied.

"I wasn't?" she said. Then: "Oh yeah, I was talking to someone. I know."

"Who?" I asked.

She could sense that something was wrong now. She was sitting next to me, close, but my body was rigid, like I couldn't stand her touch (even though I wanted it so much).

"What's up?" she asked. "Was it the fight?"

"No, it wasn't the fight," I replied. "Who were you ... *talking* to?" Boy, I could make stuff like that sound so sarcastic that it was offensive. And I did.

"Sam, if you must know," she replied, sounding irate. "Why are you in this mood all of a sudden?"

"I thought you said you were going to wait for me," I said coldly.

"Yeah, I did," she replied. "I wasn't going to stay rooted to the spot until you collected me, though. Is *that* what you're upset about?"

"What I'm upset about is you and Sam!" I replied.

"Me and S..." she began. Then it seemed to dawn on her what I meant. Her voice sounded suddenly very harsh. "What did you think me and Sam were doing?"

"I don't know, you tell me," I replied. But I did know. I knew what happened when Sam got in a room alone with a girl. And Jo was no exception.

"We were *just* talking," she said.

"Yeah, course you were," I replied, not meeting her eyes. I flicked my dog-end into the road, arcing sparks through the summer night air.

"We..." she began again, then she snapped her mouth shut. When next she spoke, her tone really hurt. "You know what? Forget it! I don't need to explain my every action to you! If you think I'm so easy that any guy can have me over in the space of three minutes, then that's fine. I guess *you* won't get that chance!"

With that, she swept off the garden wall and back into the house.

I sat in silence for a minute.

"That ... *could* have been better," I said to myself. But I was past caring. She had hurt me, and all I'd wanted to do was hurt her back. But it didn't feel good at all. I wasn't satisfied. I'd just burned the only remaining bridge between us. Now she'd never be my girlfriend, even if I wanted her. But I wasn't about to have Sam's seconds. No way.

Danny, Cathy, Sam, and Jo. All the people who were leaving me next year, who I'd wanted to stay friends with, who I'd thrown this party for; I was losing them all in the space of one night. Far from bringing us together, this party was tearing us apart. Danny and Jo probably hated my guts, and I couldn't stand Cathy or Sam right at this moment. What the hell was *happening* to us?

And suddenly I found myself grasping for a plan, something I could do, something that could pull us back from the brink, make us all friends again, bring us together. But things weren't that simple, and my beer-addled brain couldn't rise to the challenge. I felt hopeless.

Dejected, I went back inside. As I pushed open the front door, which Jo had left slightly ajar, I saw Sam coming down the stairs towards me. I didn't want to meet his eyes, but it was inevitable. I looked away, almost flinching, and walked on into the kitchen.

"Hey, Jay," said Sam, with a cheeriness that I found irritating.

I ignored him. He caught up with me.

"Talk to me," he said, a puzzled tone in his voice.

"Leave me alone," I said.

Sam laid a hand on my shoulder to stop me. I shook him off and carried on, stomping into the kitchen.

"What've I done *now*?" he asked. I didn't reply. I really couldn't face the idea of speaking to him right now. I thought that I'd choke on the words or something. How could he just stand there and pretend he *didn't* know what he'd done?

"Stuff you, then," he said as I stalked away. Yeah, and stuff you too, *friend*.

I heard him go into the lounge behind me. Probably to find Jo. I didn't look around. I kept on going, through the garden, past the people that were messing about on the grass. Someone shot a party popper with a loud bang, and streamers of colour floated through the air before me. I brushed them aside. I wasn't much in the mood for fun.

Where I ended up was in the little copse of trees at the back of my garden. It was cool and dark in there, sheltered. Nobody could see me. Nobody would find me. I didn't want to talk to anyone at the moment, I really didn't.

I picked a spot at the base of a thin treetrunk, and nestled down into the foliage. The ground was dry and hard. I was probably mucking up my trousers, but I didn't care. I leaned back against the bark, dug in my pocket and sparked up a cigarette. I had some more beers in the lounge, but I couldn't face the idea of going in and getting them. Instead, I just sucked in the tobacco smoke – which was feeling pretty rancid ten B&H's down the line, and was making the back of my throat all claggy – and gazed out of my dark hideaway at the goings-on around me.

I think I probably hit an all-time low at that point. I was really depressed. Just about nothing had gone right for me tonight. The victory over Stew was soured by Jo and Sam's betrayal. My talk with Cappo hadn't really solved any of his problems. My friend-ships were not just drifting apart but being *shattered* by the events of the night.

And just when I was ready to throw it all in and go to sleep right there amid the trees, the turbulent course of my party took another twist.

A window smashed.

I could hear it, clear as a bell; the initial crack, the splash of falling glass, the sprinkling of the finer particles on stone interspersed with occasional smashing noises as a really big chunk hit the floor. It wasn't just any window, this. It was a big window. I could tell by the sound. Something that big had to be the patio door, the big, glass door that opened on to the lower garden. The sound was like sonic doom. I – was – *dead* when my parents got back.

The smash was accompanied by chaos in the garden, as shouted accusations flew around. People were frantically trying to broadcast their innocence, blaming others. By the sounds of it, nobody knew just who had broken that window. But everybody was trying their hardest to make sure it wasn't pinned on to them.

I didn't even get up. I just sat where I was and sighed despondently. Let them sort it out themselves. Nobody would take the blame for it, so nobody would pay for it. The window was smashed; I was done for.

Then I heard the sound of running footsteps. That had me on the alert in no time at all; as far as I was concerned, running footsteps signalled guilt. Bizarrely, though, the footsteps were not coming from my garden, but from next door's garden. I told you it was a clear night. Sounds carried. Ignoring the steadily brimming chaos at my party, I scrambled to my feet and peered out from behind the trees, into the fields on the other side.

A shadowy figure was vaulting the fence at the end of Greg Thatcher's garden. He hit the grass, looked around like a hunted animal, and then sprinted off across the fields. It took me only a second of mental calculation to work out that it was an easy task to put a brick into my patio door from my neighbour's garden. And old man Thatcher was away on holiday.

In a flash, I was off in pursuit. I burst out of the trees, bellowing "Oi!" at the top of my lungs as I raced after the figure. I had thought at first that it might be Stew, but this guy had long hair in a ponytail, and was taller than Stew. He looked over his shoulder at my cry, and then began to really run, his long legs outpacing mine over the cold, steely blades of grass.

I poured on the speed – and I can be pretty quick when I want to be – but this guy was too fast. I mean he was *fast*. This chase wasn't going to last long, I knew that. But I wasn't going to give it up. I tried to concentrate on my legs, to make them run faster, to pump more quickly. Nothing worked. I watched the shadowy vandal pulling away from me, the distance making him harder and harder to see in the moonless night. I was drunk, and my heart was hammering with the effort of the sudden exercise on top of such a quantity of beer. My head felt light.

Too fast.

Then it hit me. He *was* too fast. Fast enough to be the school sprinting champion! One of the guys from class 11B. And wasn't Gary Donley growing his hair around the time he got expelled, seven-odd months ago?

And who do you think was one of Gary Donley's best friends?

Blazing with anger, I hollered at the top of my lungs. "You tell Stew I'm coming for him, Donley! And you're going down as well!"

"Yeah, right," he called back. Idiot. He'd just confirmed who he was.

"I'm coming for him!" I shouted again. And I was. I'm not a vengeful kid by nature, but Stew and his mates had overstepped the boundaries. I knew Stew was behind what had just happened, even if he wasn't here himself. A fight was one thing, but vandalizing someone's property was something else. There was no way I was going to let him get away with that. That window was going to cost me a packet, and a whole lot of grief from my parents besides. Stew had just gone too far, and I had no choice but to retaliate.

But, standing in the middle of that field at night, looking across to where the Zone was invisible behind the rise of the land, I realized that I couldn't do it alone. And I had nobody to help me.

Chapter Nine

"Danny," I said. It had taken all my courage just to speak the word. He was sitting out back, at one of the circular plastic tables, drinking a beer. He turned round at the sound of his name, saw me, and motioned for me to sit down.

"What happened to your window?" he asked, waving his hand at the empty frame of my patio door, and at the shards of glass that crunched underfoot. "Your parents are gonna go ape!"

"Yeah, I know," I said.

I had made a decision. Out there in the fields, watching Stew's mate streak away into the darkness, I had made a decision. It was all up to me. If things were bad between my friends and me, it was my job to patch it up. Hadn't I always been the peacemaker before? Well, now I needed my diplomatic skills more than ever.

I needed a team to go into the Zone. I had to get my own back on Stew. And I wasn't going without my friends. They were my team; we'd always gone in as a foursome together. It was mutual protection, for one thing. That place could be dangerous. But it was also because we were mates.

I mean, that wasn't the only reason I was doing it.

Obviously, I wanted to be on good terms with all my friends. But the smashing of my window had brought it all to a head. As if Fate had decided to personally stick a hand in, I had been suddenly given the urgent motivation to sort things out with Danny, Sam and Cappo. I didn't want to let them leave in the morning, with all the mixed feelings still hanging between us. I wanted us to leave as friends.

It was like the party was some sort of evil entity, actively trying to separate us, and I was the only one aware of it. I had to fight it, to keep us together. I had to swallow my pride and talk to Sam. I had to get Cappo motivated and get him to come along. And I had to see what kind of damage Cathy had wreaked between me and Danny by facing him.

Nobody ever said being a teenager was easy.

"So who did the window?" Danny was asking. "Are they gonna pay for it, or what?"

Danny seemed amiable enough. He certainly didn't sound mad or anything. Still, that didn't mean anything. I probably wouldn't be able to tell if he *was* mad. Observation isn't my strong suit.

"One of Stew's mates did the window," I said. "Gary Donley."

"No way!" said Danny. "Did you catch him?"

"Nope," I said. "But I'm gonna go and get 'em back."

"Damn right you are," said Danny enthusiastically. "Count me in."

"Huh?" I said thickly. I hadn't expected that.

"You going into the Zone?"

91

"Yeah," I replied. "I'm gonna catch them in their camp."

"Need some help?"

"All I can get," I said, grinning.

"Alright," said Danny. "Let's get 'em!" He held up his palm and I high-fived him, in the same stupid way I'd done earlier. Just messing around. But it felt really good.

I felt that I should leave it at that, but something inside me just wouldn't allow this thing to go unresolved. I sort of took a deep breath, then waded in.

"Umm... Cathy was talking to me earlier," I said.

"Yeah?" Danny said quizzically.

"About what she said to you, I mean," I continued.

"What she said to me?" Danny asked. "Oh, about *you*. Is that what you're talking about?"

"I think so," I replied.

Danny rocked back in his seat, swigged his beer. "She told me she fancied you," Danny said, explaining what I already knew.

I watched him warily. "Aren't you mad?"

He burst out laughing. "Mad? What for?"

A foolish grin spread across my face. "I thought ... you know ... the idea of Cathy fancying *me* when she's going out with *you*..."

"Oh, I get it," said Danny. "You thought I'd be mad at you because I'd get jealous of my girlfriend fancying my best mate."

"Something like that," I admitted. "Well, I know *I* would."

Danny laid his beer down on the table, then rested

his elbows there, leaning over towards me. I leaned closer, as well.

He whispered in my ear, an exaggerated hush-hush tone in his voice: "That's just what *she* wants me to do."

"Uh?" I kind of made a goofy noise. I wasn't following.

"You've got to get out more, Jay; it's the oldest trick in the book. She's just trying to make me jealous. It's kind of sweet, in a pathetic sort of way."

"Why? You haven't split up, have you?"

Danny grinned. "That's the irony. We hadn't, until she started this jealousy trip. It's all about attention. When she thinks I'm not paying enough attention to her, she goes off and does something like this."

"She does?"

"She's weird like that," he continued. "Believe me, I know what you guys think of her, and I'd be the first person to agree. She's absolutely nuts. Difference is, I'm used to it. And I know, when she says to me that she fancies my best mate, she just wants more attention for herself. And when I don't play along, she goes even more nuts."

Was I ever relieved.

"I don't know why she told me, or why she's making a big deal out of it." Danny leaned back. "She just *says* stuff like that. I don't reckon even she knows why. But I've been going out with her long enough to know that you just don't take any notice of half the stuff she's saying. Anyway, the whole thing's ridiculous. Why would she go for *you*," – here he nudged me jokily – "when she's lucky enough to have a stud like me?"

I laughed at that. "Is that why you fought, though?"

Danny sort of half-smiled. "Yeah. She told me that she fancied you, and I told her that it was a stupid thing to say. No offence, Jay, but if she did fancy you then it's hardly wise to tell me, is it? I told her that if she really liked you, we should break up now. I didn't mean it, just calling her bluff. Anyway, she folded – like I knew she would – and started going on about how insensitive I was and so on."

I decided not to tell Danny that Cathy had tried to kiss me in the bathroom. Probably he'd treat it in the same casual way, but it was better to be safe. Anyway, if she had done, I was sure that it wouldn't have *meant* anything. But still...

I shook my head, smiling at how silly I'd been, thinking that my best friend would be mad at me over something as petty as this. If I'd have thought about it, I should have known that Cathy is sometimes liable to say things like that; and I should have realized that Danny knows her better than I do. In the light of what he'd said, I found that I wasn't half as pissed off with Cathy as I had been before. Maybe she couldn't help being insane.

Danny caught my expression, grinning in response. "What are you smiling at, homeboy?"

I shrugged in exasperation. "Why *do* you go out with her, Danny?"

"It's something to do," he replied, knowing how

that answer irritated me and relishing his moment of gentle revenge.

One down.

So everything was cool with Danny. But I still couldn't pluck up the courage to face Sam yet, not after what he and Jo had done to me. Instead, I went for the easier option: Cappo. I stopped in the kitchen – where the bright Formica worktops were losing their red criss-cross pattern under an avalanche of empty beer cans and fag-ends – and made two cups of strong coffee. The smell of hollow tinnies made me desperate for a beer myself, but I knew that I couldn't. I was already wrecked, and I needed to be sharp if I was going to go back into the Zone after all this time. One coffee was for me, to sober me up a bit. The other was for Cappo.

He was still in the bathroom when I found him, lying in a heap, his mouth slightly open and a runnel of drool depending from the corner of his mouth, hanging just above the carpet as if unwilling to touch the floor. He was asleep. He must have been zonked.

I locked the door behind me, then hunkered down next to him. It seemed almost a shame to wake him; I knew he wouldn't appreciate it. He was probably too drunk to be any help in the Zone, but I just couldn't go without him. I remembered the Zone Running we did before. Always the four of us. We each took positions, planned it out like a military exercise; Danny was point man, me and Sam were flankers, and

Cappo was the rearguard. Just like it was outside the Zone; each of us providing something on which the others relied. If one of us drifted, the whole thing collapsed. Without Cappo, it would be incomplete.

I'd made up my mind. He was coming, even if I had to carry him.

I shook him by the shoulder. First gently – which produced no response – then more violently. He groaned, feebly trying to push my hand away, but I wouldn't give up. Eventually, the disturbance became too much for him, and his eyelids peeled back blearily.

"Whaaat?" he sighed dismally, unhappy at having been woken up. His head probably felt like a herd of wildebeest had taken a dump in it, and I imagined his mouth tasted like stale phlegm. I was sympathetic; I'd been to Hangover City before. The best cure is to sleep it off, but of course, I wasn't about to let him do that.

"You've got a mission, Cappo," I said. "Here, I brought you some coffee."

I helped him sit up, then handed him the steaming mug. He took a sip, his whole body radiating feebleness as if it was hoping that I'd leave him alone so it could get back to sleep.

"You'll be lucky if you think I'm going anywhere," he murmured. His throat sounded rough.

"I'm always lucky," I said. As if.

Cappo frowned at the pulsating thud in his skull.

"What do you *want*, Jay?" he bleated.

"I want you to wake up."

"Leave me alone," he said. "I'm too pissed to wake up."

I smiled apologetically. "I'm gonna sit here and hassle you all night if you try and go back to sleep."

"What, did I commit some kind of crime in a past life?" he moaned. "What did I do to deserve you?"

That was what I liked about Cappo. Even feeling as bad as he was, he could still summon up a bit of dark humour now and again. I decided it was time to stop messing about. "We're gonna go back into the Zone, Cappo. I need you there."

Cappo managed a weak laugh. "You must be out of your box. I couldn't make it down the stairs right now. I'm not going into the Zone."

"You have to," I insisted.

"What for?" Cappo asked.

I explained to him what had happened.

"So go with Danny," he said. "You don't need me. I wouldn't be any good anyhow."

"You've got to come, Cappo," I persisted. "We need the old team. We can't go in without you."

"Tough," he replied. I opened my mouth to argue, but he stopped me. "No, Jay, listen to me. I'm not going into the Zone. I don't even reckon I can stand, let alone run. That place is bloody dangerous, and I'm too wrecked to take it right now. I'm not going along just to make up the numbers. Take Thunderchunk instead."

"He'll never be such a good rearguard as you."

"You'll cope."

I sat back, temporarily defeated. Cappo watched

me warily, taking a sip of his coffee, waiting to see if I was going to try anything else. I could tell he was hoping I'd go away. I racked my brains for some kind of way to persuade him, something to motivate him.

What the hell, I thought. I'll tell him what's *really* bothering me.

"I'm scared, Cappo," I said. "I'm scared of losing everybody. You, Sam, Danny; it just seems like we're drifting apart. I threw this party to try and keep us together, but it's all going to pieces. Sam's being a bastard, and Cathy's gone loopy again, and ... I can't leave it like this, okay?"

"You're being stupid, Jay," said Cappo. "Sam and Danny aren't gonna forget just because they don't go to the same school."

"Yeah, you *say* that," I replied. "But they might. Not straight away, but over time. I just feel ... it seems it isn't gonna *last*. And that's why I want to go back into the Zone. The old team, like we *used* to be. All together, relying on each other. Like with Ian Huntingdon. You know? You remember?"

Cappo grinned. "Yeah, I do. They were fun times."

"So let's do it again! For me ... for us. Let's remind ourselves what it was like! What it was like to rely on your *friends*, without any of this crap about school-work and girlfriends and jobs getting in the way!"

"You think that's gonna stop us falling out of touch?" asked Cappo. He sighed and gave me a long-suffering look. "I think you're crazy. I think all this stuff about us drifting apart is just you being para-noid."

98

I was crestfallen.

"But..." he continued, in a tone that suggested that he couldn't believe what he was about to say, "if it means that much to you, I'll go in with you."

"Al*right*," I whooped, slightly over-enthusiastic. "Thanks, Cappo. I really wanted you to come."

"Just don't ever ask me for anything again," he warned.

"No problem," I replied, getting up and backing off towards the door. "I'm forever in your debt."

"Come and get me when you're ready," he said. "I'm gonna try and sober up."

"I'll be back," I promised, unlocking the door and disappearing through it. Without Cappo, the whole thing would have seemed artificial. But now ... well, the plan was on track. Only Sam remained. The hardest one.

"*I hate your guts, Jay!*" Cappo cried good-naturedly after me, as I scampered down the stairs like a five-year-old.

Talking to Sam was going to be rough, but I had to do it, if the team was to be complete. My skin felt clammy as I went looking for him. What was I going to say? When it came to the crunch, could I really swallow my pride and ask him to come along? He knew that I was mad with him about something, because I'd given him the cold shoulder earlier. I suspected that Jo had filled him in on the details. It made me grimace to think of those two talking behind my back.

I checked most of the house, but he wasn't there. That meant he was in the lounge. I didn't feel up to trying to talk him round with half the world listening in, but I guessed that I didn't have any choice. I pushed open the door to the lounge and went inside.

The Orbital CD was playing again, very quietly. Someone was sprawled across my sofa, asleep. The crush of people on the floor had thinned out considerably. Most of the people who were going had already gone, now that it was past midnight. Others had wandered away to find a cosy place to sleep, or indulge in some less savoury activities.

Sam was there. With Jo.

They saw me as I came in. I almost flinched away from the sight of them sitting together. Jo looked disgusted at the sight of me, an expression crossing her face that wounded me deeper than any insult could have done. Sam hesitated for a moment, said something to Jo, then got up and crossed the room to meet me. Jo looked away.

"Sam," I said, in curt acknowledgement.

"Jay," he replied, likewise.

This was gonna be hard. I physically could not stand the sight of him, knowing what he had done. I was just drawing breath to say something, with no idea what it was, when Sam unexpectedly made it easier for me.

"Danny came and talked to me," he said. "He was going on about a trip into the Zone."

"That was what I came to talk to you about," I said, unable to keep a tone of sullenness from my voice.

"You're going there to get Gary Donley?"

"We're going there to get all of them," I replied.

Sam looked at me levelly with his dark brown eyes. He seemed to deliberate for a moment, then he said, "Fine. I'll come."

And that was that. He turned away and went and sat down with Jo again. I couldn't leave the lounge fast enough, to get them out of my sight.

I felt weird. Nothing had been resolved. We were still at odds with each other. It was the most stilted conversation I had ever had, yet . . . Sam was coming. The team was assembled. All four of us.

This was going to be some strange kind of mission.

Chapter Ten

We crested the shallow mound at the end of the field and there was the Zone below us, spreading away like a shattered stone jigsaw. Danny sucked in his breath melodramatically as we looked across fifty square acres of derelict buildings, broken walls and rubble. It was darker than anything down there; the dawn was still a good few hours off, and the sun hadn't even begun to tinge the sky yet.

"Check it out, kids," Danny said. "Just like I remember it."

"I can't believe you talked me into this," Cappo said. But he wasn't moaning, he was just sort of lodging a protest. Secretly, I could tell he was up for it. He was so plastered, he probably thought he was invincible anyway, now that the walk across the fields had freshened off some of the tiredness from his body.

I looked at Sam. His face was in shadow, but I could tell by the twin windows of light reflecting from his eyes that he was looking back at me. Silently, he turned his face away.

Danny was already tracking it down the grass verge, towards the chain-link fence. I hefted my backpack and followed him down. It was actually

Danny's backpack, but I'd been designated the official mule for this journey, so I was lugging the equipment. There wasn't much, but it was pretty wearing to carry for a long distance. Danny had never got mule duty yet; he was the point man, and he relied on speed and stealth to keep the rest of us out of trouble.

Cappo slithered down after me, almost losing his footing several times on the slight incline. He kept making funny little "Whoa ... whoa..." noises all the way down, pinwheeling his arms in a parody of balancing. At least, I think it was a parody. I couldn't tell if he was taking the piss or not.

Now Cappo is strictly the rearguard – the guy who stops people sneaking up behind you by keeping his eyes skinned for ambushes – so he should have gone after Sam, not before. But we were still outside the boundaries of the Zone, and military discipline wasn't yet in effect. The state we were in, though, any kind of discipline was asking a lot. Sam was still swigging a beer as he trolled down after us towards the fence.

"Wa-hoo!" Danny howled, knitting his fingers through the mesh of the fence and rattling it noisily. "We're back!"

I flinched at the noise, even though we were probably too far away for anyone to hear. But Danny was really charged about being back here, and I was hardly going to shut him up after I'd asked him to come, was I?

"They still haven't got round to putting that razor-tape up on the top of this fence," Danny said, grabbing my arm. "They were gonna do that, what, four years ago? Can you believe these guys?"

"Saves you lacerating your arms on the way over," I said. "What are you complaining about?"

"I don't know," said Danny, grinning. "I guess I expected more this time around. You know, I expected the Zone to be a bit harder."

"You know what it's like in there," I said. "This time it's pitch-dark and we're all wasted. That enough of a handicap for you?"

"It'll do me fine," said Danny, then jammed his toe into the fence and boosted himself up the mesh, dragging himself over the top and dropping down the other side, landing heavily. He turned to face me through the barrier, his face expectant, as if he had just dared me to follow. Sam leaped up beside me, threw himself over in one effortless pull, and climbed down the other side. I felt a sudden surge of resentment. Was he trying to get one up on me or something, by going first, by showing he wasn't afraid?

Cappo looked daunted as he surveyed the fence, then laid his hands on the mesh. I stopped him. "Uh-uh, Cappo. Remember formation? From now on, we go as we went before."

Cappo stepped back unsteadily, nodding to himself. I tossed the bag of junk over the top of the fence, where Danny caught it. Then I launched myself upward and forward, grabbing my fingers around the thick chain mesh near the top lip, and dug in with my feet, scrabbling up the fence – which was bending

inwards with my weight like a rope-ladder does –
until I got one arm over the top. I boosted with my
feet, rolled over the fence, and hung off down the
other side. I dropped the last few inches. My shoes hit
ground a little sooner than I had expected; I suppose
I'd grown since the last time I came here.

Cappo tried to climb the fence slowly. This is
generally not a good idea – it's a lot better to fly up it
and let the momentum of your jump carry you over
the top – but Cappo obviously didn't feel like moving
fast today. I watched his face as he clambered up the
mesh, which was flexing to and fro unforgivingly
beneath his feet. I began to feel a little guilty; should I
really have dragged him out on this mission when he
was barely sober enough to walk, let alone climb?
But somehow, he made it. He got hung up on the top
lip for a while, plucking up the courage to swing his
weight over, but in the end he did. He crashed down
next to me, his legs buckling under him, and fell
backwards on to the grass.

"Nice landing," said Danny.

"Thanks," Cappo replied, looking up at the stars,
which were no doubt pinwheeling around his field of
vision.

"You alright?" asked Sam, offering a hand to
Cappo.

Cappo grabbed it and stood up. "Yup, okay," he
said. "No points for style, though."

"Depends," Sam returned. "You'd have done better if you hadn't gone for that half-pike on the way
down."

Danny and Cappo laughed, but I wasn't in the mood to laugh at anything Sam said, so I kept quiet.

We pushed on to the Zone proper. Soon, the grass beneath our feet came to an abrupt end as a long kerb stretched out of the darkness, cutting across our path. It was the dividing line. Beyond that point, there was only stone and concrete, acres and acres of it. Buildings hulked all around, rotting shells of factories and warehouses that hid a thousand secret places.

There was one thing about the Zone that hadn't changed; wherever you looked, you still found yourself glimpsing dimly-lit shapes through the cracks in the walls, distorted goblin-faces that glared balefully as you passed. Of course, they were just bits of junk or something, but even so, the feeling was disconcerting. At night, this whole place was eerie. Like a graveyard, except that the dead weren't people but buildings.

"So where are they?" Sam asked Danny.

"Like I know," Danny replied sarcastically. "Jay?"

"Beats me," I replied. "You're point man."

"You don't *know*?" Sam blurted.

I cast him a withering look. At least, I hoped it was. Have you noticed how only girls can wither with any kind of skill?

"They've got a fire going. How hard is it going to be to see them at night? We'll smell it a mile off, any-way."

"Great," replied Sam. "So we wander about all night."

"Don't be so gloomy," Danny replied. "We just make high ground and look for the glow of the fire. Where's your initiative?"

"We didn't see the fire from the top of the hill," Cappo pointed out.

"Did you look?" I asked, getting a little pissed off with all this dissension.

"No," Cappo admitted.

"There you are, then." I was smug.

"Are we gonna go, or what?" Danny asked. "Come on. I'm point, you guys follow. Let's move out!"

Danny and me loved all these little military Americanisms. We'd ripped off thousands of them from all the Schwarzenegger movies. It just didn't sound cool if you weren't saying things like: "Incoming!" and "Watch your six!" and all that kind of stuff. I mean, it's not like I'm into the Army or anything like that but in the Zone, you know, you've got to play your part. It wouldn't be half so exciting if we were just sloping around the place like it was just an average set of streets. This place was a war zone! And we were Zone Runners!

We trekked towards the heart of the Zone. On the outskirts, it was relatively safe to travel down the roadways, because you could see a good way ahead and people rarely hung out there. Closer in, it became necessary to slip off the road and take the more twisting paths between the buildings. I mean, I know I said the Zone was a big place, but then a lot of people go there; towards the middle, you've got a fair chance of running into somebody and being seen if you're not on your guard.

You might wonder why a town like mine has so many brain-damage victims on the back doorstep, but the fact is that it *doesn't*. They come from miles around to this place. No cops, no authority; it was party heaven for them. Lucky us. I suppose what I'm saying is, if we got seen, some guys might try and beat us up just for the hell of it. You can do anything you want in the Zone. That makes it dangerous for us.

Stew and the gang were baby thugs. I suppose they were tolerated because Stew's older brother was ticking off the days till jail, but I knew that the older kids wouldn't let them in on their action. So I reckoned they'd be camped a little way away from the centre of the Zone. I tried to think of all the places that would be suitable for a bonfire around there. I began to rack my brains.

"We're coming up to the NoGo area," Danny whispered up ahead. "You can see the Square from here."

We caught up with him, silently climbing up some short stacks of wooden forklift palettes and looking over the high brick wall. Between a couple of silent factories, beat-box music drifted over to us. Some kind of unrecognizable chart gumph; the usual mix of soul and rap. I could see a gang of people down there, in the glow of a bonfire; they were swigging two-litre plastic bottles of beer and doing whatever substances they could get their hands on. Those were the guys we really wanted to avoid. The zombies.

The Square was the unofficial central point of the Zone. I mean, it wasn't the *geographic* centre, but it was the most convenient place for people to assemble, and over the years it had become the only place to be where the Zone was concerned. Sort of like the Copacabana for derelicts. This was where the bad guys came to get drunk and high.

The Square was originally a paved courtyard between three office buildings, with one side open to the road. Because of this, it had loads of places to sit around, and the central fountain – now dry – provided the perfect place to erect bonfires.

Stew wouldn't be there. But he wouldn't be far away.

"Come on, let's go around," I said. I had an idea that they would be on this side of the Square – I mean, we'd already walked a fair way from my house, and I knew that Gary Donley wouldn't bother to slog it for miles just to chuck a brick through my window – and there were only a couple of suitable places nearby. I didn't know the Zone that well, but the few times I'd been through, I had remembered the trips fairly well. Adrenaline does that to you, I reckon.

"Any idea where we're going?" asked Danny.

"You know where there's that car park, over that way?"

"Yeah. You reckon they're there?"

I scratched the back of my neck. "Well, there's a lot of flat tarmac to build a fire on, and there's that big grass verge close by. Space enough to pitch a tent, park a car, whatever. I mean, they've gotta have *somewhere* to get it on, don't they? The ground'll be a little uncomfortable."

"And it's right next to the loading bay of some truck yard," said Cappo, suddenly bright. "And there's tons of these around" – here he rapped his knuckles on the wooden forklift palettes we were kneeling on – "which they could burn. At least, there were when I was there before."

"Sounds good to me," said Sam.

So it was agreed. We crept back down the palettes and onward. It was easy to keep covered around this area; most of the factories were so gutted by the fire that had created the Zone that we could nip right through them through the holes in the walls. It was pretty treacherous underfoot, with sliding bits of wood and glass threatening to send you flying any minute. I didn't fancy falling down inside one of these factories; you were liable to get a rusty nail stuck in your palm and get tetanus.

I caught myself. Why was I worrying about such *stupid* things? *Tetanus?* Right now I should be more worried about getting my head stoved in.

So there we were, picking our way through some old factory, with the sky clearly visible through the huge, ragged holes in the roof, high above us. Half-standing walls leaned around aimlessly, deepening the already impenetrable shadows. I felt a crawling chill seep down from my shoulders. This was danger territory. The dark corners seemed to harbour menace.

Then I heard a hiss from up ahead, and saw Danny waving at us from the doorway. It took me a second to realize why he was gesturing; *someone was coming!*

"Get into cover!" I whispered urgently, seeing that Danny was already concealing himself behind an empty gas canister. We scrambled for the cover of the broken walls. My eyes fell on a doorway – well, it was more of a door *frame*, as there were only a few bricks left holding it up – that led into what must have once been an office. Grabbing Cappo's arm (Sam could fend for himself), I led him through it, and we crouched down behind a protective screen of bricks just as the sound of voices floated in from outside. I was just thinking that we'd all got out of sight when I heard a scuffling of sliding glass and wood nearby, frighteningly loud. It was Sam, who had flung himself behind some crates at the last second and knocked loose some debris in the process.

The voices outside stopped. So did my breathing.

"Hear that?" one of them asked the other. A high, reedy male voice, but still unmistakably belonging to someone a lot older than us.

"Dunno," replied the other. His voice was more throaty. "What was it?"

"Dunno," echoed the first. "Hey, anybody in here?"

His call met silence. Me and Cappo exchanged glances, and I could tell that he, like me, was trying to will his heart to stop beating because it seemed too loud.

"If there's someone at it in here, jus' tell us and we'll bugger off," said the higher voice.

No reply. Of course.

"Prob'ly wasn't anything," said the other guy. I thought of all the horror films I'd seen when that line was immediately followed by the speaker being gruesomely murdered, and it brought a smile to my face. Yeah, I wasn't too frightened to smile. But I was still pretty damn scared. I mean, you never knew what you got with the zombies. Some of them were *way* nuts, and some of them were just interested in getting a kick. If luck was with you, you'd be okay; but if you met one of the nutters, you were screwed big-time.

Stealth was the key at the moment. If we were caught, our strike on Stew would be ruined. And I found myself thinking, no matter how nasty this place was, I didn't want it to be over yet. Out here, I could forget about Jo and Cathy and all that. The old heart-pounding excitement was back. Damn, I'd missed this place!

"Cobber's getting on my tits something rotten," the lower-voiced speaker said. I heard the rattle of a zip somewhere, then the steady splashing of urine as one of them relieved himself against a wall. I remembered Danny, in his – frankly unwise – hiding place behind the gas canister near the door. I pictured the guy pissing on Danny accidentally and almost began to laugh. Cappo laid his finger roughly across my lips.

"Ah, I know. He's always on about that bloody bike of his."

"Yeah. Like, great, we really want to *know*, Cobber. Tell us *more* about your *won*derful Yamaha."

"It's prob'ly some cheesy 10cc thing with, like, a top speed of seven miles per hour."

"Yeah," said the deeper voice, pausing to take a swig of his beer. I figured that drinking beer and having a piss at the same time would require more dexterity than they possessed, so it must have been the higher-voiced one who was going to the toilet. "But to hear him talk about it, you'd think it was a Harley-bloody-Davidson."

The unwavering drill of urine dried to a trickle. There was a rustle of material – probably the guy's bubble-jacket – then a harsh zipping sound as he whipped his flies up. Doing it that fast, he was taking his life in his hands, I thought – and immediately felt another surge of irrational mirth. I was really enjoying eavesdropping on these two, especially as they didn't seem to have a clue we were there.

"I swear, if he goes on about it any more, I'll deck him out," the deep voice continued.

"Nah, you'll have Jonno and that lot on your back then."

A sigh. "True. I wish the sod hadn't come."

"It's only for tonight. He's off back to Bristol tomorrow."

"What a shame," came the reply, heavily sarcastic.

"I could give him – hey, who's that behind there?"

"What?"

My heart sank as I heard the words. "There's a kid behind that canister!"

Danny broke cover and ran, pelting across the factory floor. He could have gone for the door nearby, the one that we were going to go through, but it's never a good idea to run in the direction of the enemy. If those two guys had come from out there, there was no telling how many more of them there were. No, he went running back the way we had come, I could tell by his footsteps. The two guys shouted after him – more surprised than angry, I think – but Danny had the edge on their sodden reactions, and he was halfway out before they even started to chase him. Whether they were psychos or just stoneheads, Danny wasn't hanging around to find out.

I heard a curse and a crash as one of them fell over, losing his footing amid the debris of the factory floor. I don't reckon Danny even looked back. He was straight on out of there. They never had a chance. Like I said before, Danny's got a certain natural style about him, and that extends as far as making him a pretty fast runner, too. I don't think Danny's street-cred would allow him to be disfigured by a hammering.

"Little sod," the low-voiced one said. "Ah, I've buggered up my hand. Shit, there's a needle down there."

"It get you?"

"Nah."

"Dunno what the skanky little rodent was doing here anyhow. Listening in on us or something."

"Forget it," said the other. "Let's get back. Damn, look at all the crap I got wedged in my palm."

114

The voices faded without my ever having seen the owners. But I didn't really care about them any more. I was worried about only one thing: where Danny had gone. The four of us had become three. We'd lost our point man. We could only dig in and hope he'd come back to us. But what if he didn't?

Chapter Eleven

"There they are," Sam whispered.

"Right where you said they'd be, Jay," Cappo replied. "Nice one."

I cast a triumphant look at Sam. It was pretty childish of me, but I didn't care. He caught the glance, but ignored it.

Him and Jo, him and Jo. Why couldn't I get it out of my mind?

We were crouching behind a cluster of old metal skips, each about seven or eight feet high and stacked with refuse that had long since decomposed. Printed on the side, in flaking black paint against the tarnished yellow, was the name of the firm that supplied them. Bunsons or Ronsons or something. I couldn't tell. Not that I cared, anyway.

Not very far away, there was a fierce blaze going, around which were clustered several shadowy figures. The bonfire was still in its prime – they'd stacked it high – and the people sitting around it couldn't get too close because of the intensity of the heat. The flickering glow cast shivering shadows across the tarmac, illuminating the faces around it. I recognized them all. And there, with a cigarette drooping from his mouth and a bottle of beer in his hand, was Stew.

"Where's Donley?" asked Sam.

"Gary Donley?" I replied, stupidly. Frankly, I was surprised that he'd spoken to me.

"No, you crip. Regina Donley the Third of the Queen's Airborne Corps," he replied, his words dripping scorn.

I suppose I deserved that. "On the far side," I replied. I wasn't rising to the bait. We'd already lost one Zone Runner; if Sam walked, it would effectively mean the mission was over. I wasn't going to start laying into him here.

"Oh, yeah," he replied sullenly.

Danny hadn't come back. We had waited in that factory for what seemed like an hour (but which was probably closer to fifteen minutes; nobody had a watch) and there had been no sign of him. I mean, I could understand it if he had been chased away for some distance by those guys – it's very easy to get lost in the Zone at night – but they'd barely bothered to pursue him to the door. I wondered why he hadn't come back. We all did. And it worried us.

"I don't like this," I said. "It doesn't feel right doing it without Danny. We were always *four*. That's how we work.'

"Can't be helped," Sam said. "Danny could be anywhere. He'll be okay; but we've gotta do this.'

"Why are *you* so keen, anyway?" I asked, faintly accusatory.

"Listen, Jay," Cappo interrupted before Sam could reply. "The best way we can find Danny again is to carry on with the plan. He knows where we were headed. He'll either go back home or make for this place."

"And what if he's caught?" I replied.

"Then we go get him," Cappo replied.

Anyway, there we were, watching the mob around the bonfire. And I found myself thinking that we were lucky Danny never got mule duty; I still had all the kit with me. It was a hastily assembled pack of stuff, grabbed at short notice from my house, but there was the potential for a lot of chaos in Danny's rucksack. And that was what we intended to create. We weren't going down there to beat them up or anything. That was for people with less imagination than we had. No, we wanted to frighten them, to humiliate them, to let them know that they'd been defeated. Maybe they'd try and hit my house again in reprisal, but I reckoned they wouldn't. Too many people had seen Stew outside the party; he'd never get away with it.

But here in the Zone, you could get away with anything.

I rummaged past a few cans of barbecued beans and a fat ball of twine and grabbed a handful of capbangers. These were gloriously easy to construct – you just folded your strip of paper caps down the centre to release the tiny charges of gunpowder, then folded them over a few times and Sellotaped them together, along with a fuse made of a strip of elastic band – and they were pretty loud, too.

Sam stopped me. I felt a tiny burst of resentment.

"There's no point just mowing in there with all that

stuff," Sam said. "There's loads of them and three of us. We need an escape route, and we need to be able to stop them following."

"Booby traps!" Cappo grinned.

I had to admit that Sam had a point. Fortunately, the bag was loaded with enough stuff to cope with just about any eventuality. We'd grabbed a load of stuff back at my house, assembling all the old tools of our trade. Some of them seemed painfully outdated and juvenile now, but hey, they'd still *work*. And besides, they were the weapons of our childhood, of a time when things weren't so complicated. It was strangely comforting to be carrying them again.

We scouted back a bit, working out a route that would take us back to the main road. From there, we could peg it all the way home in a straight line. It was a bit exposed, but if the plan went well, then there wouldn't be anybody following us by then. The route was pretty tortuous, but that was the idea; we were hoping to throw off the pursuit after we had struck. If they caught one of us, they'd be awfully mad. Especially after what we were planning.

Still there was no sign of Danny. Surely he hadn't quit on us and flaked out back to my house? No way. Then maybe he was in real trouble...

"We *can't* go looking for him now," said Sam, when I suggested this to everyone. "We've got no idea where he is. Let's just get these guys and get out of here."

I thought about protesting, but he was right. It was too early to write Danny off yet, that was for sure.

"One thing, though," said Sam. "I want Gary Donley."

Cappo grinned. "Yeah, you owe him one alright," he said.

"Hang on," I said, clambering shakily over a pile of crates on our way back along the escape route. "It was *my* window he broke. What's going on?"

Sam didn't seem about to reply, so Cappo did instead. "You know about Sam and his pulling powers, right?" he said. "Girls just fall at his feet, yeah?"

Boy, Cappo had the talent of saying the wrong thing. I tried to remember that he didn't know what had happened between me and Sam and Jo, but it still rankled something awful. Fortunately, Cappo didn't expect me to agree verbally. The evidence was overwhelming.

"Well, remember that blonde he pulled at Tito's on Friday?" Cappo continued mischievously.

"Shut up, Cappo," Sam warned, but Cappo wasn't having any of that.

"What about her?" I asked expectantly.

"And you know how Sam said he'd chucked her after a few hours?"

"Yeah?"

"Cappo!" Sam growled.

"He didn't chuck her," Cappo replied, bursting out laughing. "She sodded off with Gary Donley while he was in the toilet!"

I couldn't help it. I just cracked up. Me and Cappo laughed until we just about ruptured ourselves, with

Sam standing by with the most pissed-off expression on his face that you ever saw. Every time I looked at him, scowling at the floor, I laughed even harder. I could see he was getting really riled, like he was going to punch one of us or something if we didn't shut up, but I didn't care at all. It was such beautiful revenge.

But then, something happened. I don't know why, but it seemed kind of important to me at the time. Or maybe that's just how I remember it. Anyway, what happened was that Sam stopped scowling. A smile touched the corner of his lips, and his face took on *that* expression. You know the one I mean: the kind of one you get when some teacher's shouting at you and your mate is pulling faces at him behind his back. The one where you can't laugh but you can't *help* it. Then his resistance broke, and he began to laugh, too. First chuckles, then real long, hard laughs, like the rest of us.

It was dangerous to laugh that loud in the Zone. But right then, it didn't matter. We were all doubled over, just killing ourselves with laughter, and suddenly things really seemed to be alright between us again.

And in that moment of clarity I realized that it wasn't worth chucking away a friendship like I had with Sam because of a girl. *Any* girl. Because girls come and go, but your friends are for ever.

I looked at Sam, and he looked at me, and I realized that I'd forgiven him. I can't stay mad at people for long anyway. I didn't say as much, but we both knew.

Instead, I said: "Let's go crash their party. It's payback time." And I knew that it was going to be alright.

Chapter Twelve

The scene was set.

It had taken us about half an hour, maybe longer, but the whole plan was worked out now. Whether it was going to come off as we intended was another matter altogether. Well, whatever. We had done the best we could. Right then I wasn't all that bothered if the plan didn't work at all; it had been so good to get back into the Zone with my friends that I didn't care. I knew that they felt the same too. They had that glint of excitement in their eyes. Even Cappo (who had sobered up considerably by now) was looking sharp. I was just sorry that Danny wasn't here. But, point man or no point man, we had to go on.

"Okay, enough messing about," I said. "Let's do it."

Most of the gang were hanging around the bonfire, sitting on the tarmac of the car park, surrounded by cans of beer, packets of rolling tobacco and ... well, other stuff. Don't get thinking that it was only the zombies in the Square that were getting whacked out. There were about three tents pitched nearby, on the wide, flat grass verge. And like I said, they weren't intending to *sleep* there. All around, the firelight danced across the empty windows of the burned-out buildings.

I went out wide, skirting the car park, well beyond the range of the firelight. It was hard to see anything, what with my night vision totally destroyed by staring at the fire for too long, but I kept low to the ground and crept slowly towards the tents on the far side. I was getting the more dangerous job, because the tents were quite a way away, and I'd have to pelt it to catch up with the others before Stew's mob got hold of me.

At least Cappo had the bag of tricks now; I had insisted that he take it, because he had the shortest distance to run and it was heavy enough to slow me down. I was left with a handful of cap-bangers and my lighter. It doesn't matter if you smoke or not, a cigarette lighter must be the handiest thing ever created and no self-respecting teenager should be without one. You can use it to light other people's tabs (primarily girls'); you can start fires with it; you can roast small insects and spiders (sickos only, obviously); you can pour lighter fluid on your finger and ignite it (I've seen people do that and then wonder why it hurts. No kidding); and of course, you can use it to light fuses, which was pretty much what I intended to do.

I crept up on the tents, and from what I could see, it was pretty obvious that only one of them was occupied. Inside, some bloke and a girl were talking. She was giggling coyly at something he said. The other two tents were silent, with their flaps hanging open. Good, there was only one target. That made my job easier.

Sam was watching from behind the big, rusty skip. I couldn't see him in the darkness, and he couldn't see me, but I knew he was out there, waiting for my signal. At the first sign of a flame from my lighter – which would be easily visible in the darkness – the plan was to commence. I remembered something Hannibal used to say in the A-Team: "I love it when a plan comes together." I don't know why, but right at that moment, I felt like I was poised on the brink of doing the coolest thing *ever*. Cooler even than Ian Huntingdon's keyring. This was going to be the best piece of Zone Running in history.

I spun the wheel of the lighter and the flame snapped into life. Hastily, knowing that I was suddenly visible to everyone around the fire, I touched the flame to the fuses of a cluster of cap-bangers that I had clenched in my fist. Then, slipping the lighter back in my pocket, I waited as the elastic bands burned down a little. With one deep breath, I ran to the occupied tent, yanked up the zipper violently and tossed the lit bangers into the darkness within. "What the hell—" began a gruff voice, but he was cut short by the sudden rip of explosions inside the tent. The girl who was with him screamed, and he swore at the top of his lungs. In the confines of the tent, the explosions must have been deafening.

With a fierce grin on my face, I was pegging it through the darkness, unheeding the danger of tripping as I raced towards where Cappo was waiting. As I ran, I heard a dull *whoomp* to my left, and I saw the party that was huddling around the fire erupt into chaos, falling backwards with their hands before their eyes. Some of them were running around, shaking their limbs, trying to fling off the muck that coated them. You'd think it was napalm, not barbecued beans; Sam had tossed a can on to the bonfire, and pressurized cans have a tendency to explode when heated violently.

Another *whoomp* as the second can of beans distributed its payload all over the distressed gang. I laughed out loud as I saw them, flailing around madly, rolling on the ground like idiots. But I didn't have time to hang about and admire Sam's handiwork; already I could hear the guy in the tent scrambling out of it and swearing loudly at my back. He was plenty mad, I can tell you; I just hoped that he wasn't as fast a runner as Gary Donley was. I put my head down and made speed out of there.

Our escape route was through a narrow alley entrance, behind the set of skips that we'd been hiding behind when we first found Stew and the gang. It was there that Cappo was waiting with a pair of old metal dustbins that we'd spotted nearby, slightly scorched but still serviceable. I flew towards it, just behind Sam (who had attracted a pretty healthy following of his own, now that the guys around the campfire had worked out where the mysterious attack was coming from) and we both wheeled sharply around the edge of the skips and rushed into the enclosed alley.

It took only a moment for Cappo to shove the bins into place as we passed. The alley entrance was, as I said, pretty narrow, and the big metal skips shielded it from view. Any second now, someone was going to come pelting around that corner, straight for the alley where we'd gone; and I didn't much fancy their chances of stopping in time before they hit those bins.

Either way, we weren't sticking around to watch the fun. We aimed to put as much distance between us and them as possible. In fact, me and Sam hadn't stopped running; but we were gracious enough to slow down a little so that Cappo could catch up. Credit to him, though; he was the most blasted of all of us, and he managed to scoot down the alley at a pretty fair whack without falling over anything. I imagined that the adrenaline was sharpening him up. I know that was the case with me.

On that thought, however, it was only then that I realized just how bloody dangerous this whole plan was. We'd missed one slight element in our planning. Y'see, then we had been *walking* along the escape route, sidestepping debris quite easily; we hadn't considered what it would be like to run along an alley strewn with glass and bits of rock at full speed in deep darkness. The whole thing was scary as hell. It seemed like I was only surviving by virtue of an instinct that I couldn't even pin down, one that told me where to put my feet before my eyes had even registered the obstacle. I don't know how we were doing it, but we were *doing* it.

Behind us, I heard a glorious crash as two metal bins full of trash collided brutally with someone's upper thighs, sending them spilling over in a jumble of arms, legs and litter. I whooped at the top of my voice, letting them know that they'd been caught out. The bins were clattering all over the place as the victim fought to extract himself from the mess, and others tried to clamber past him to get to us.

"It's a dead-end alley!" one of them shouted. Stew. I recognized his voice. "Get 'em!"

He was right, it *was* a dead-end alley. But of course, we had it covered. We weren't stupid. As we reached the wall at the end, there was a ramp made of several planks, supported by crates underneath. At least, *one* plank was; the one on the far left. If anyone else tried to step on any of the others, the planks would collapse under their feet. Were we good or what?

Sam raced up the safe plank, launched himself up the wall and pulled himself over. He always was the athletic one. I let Cappo go next, figuring that he might need some help if his balance didn't hold out; but he surprised me by flinging himself over with almost suicidal zeal. I scrambled up last, hoisting myself over and dropping on to the pre-cleared patch of tarmac below.

Another alley, this one almost knee-high in rubble that had fallen from the roof above. In the glow of the night sky, it looked impassable, hunks of rock limned in dark blue. It would be hard going to get over all that rock. That was why *we* weren't going to. But Stew and his mates were.

We could hear them charging down the alley behind the wall, shouting at the tops of their voices now, raising a proper ruckus. The little surprise of the bins that we had left them had really got them angry. They knew now that this wasn't just a joke, that we were really thumbing our noses at them. I didn't give much for our chances if they caught us, that much was for sure.

Sam led the way, ducking down and crawling through a ragged hole in the wall to our left. We had carefully concealed it from view by piling up rubble against one side, so it was almost invisible unless you knew where to look. We scrabbled hastily inside and ran along the interior of the building – which was relatively clear – with the windows to our right blurring along like the edge of a cinema film reel. We could probably have run off through the factory at that moment, and taken another route out of the Zone. Certainly, it would have taken Stew and that lot a while to work out where we'd gone. But we weren't satisfied yet, and we still had a little more retribution to deal out to our enemies.

The windows ran parallel to the alley, and there was a door at the end. We'd already propped it open in preparation. We nipped through that, so now we were at the far end of the alley, with the big stretch of highly unstable debris between us and Stew's mob. When they came over that wall, they'd think that we had run over the rubble, not gone along a side route; and they'd try to do the same. That should be a laugh.

We heard an explosive splintering of wood and a cry as the lead pursuer put his foot through the loose planking that we had laid up against the last alley wall. Judging by the follow-up sounds, somebody else ran into the back of him, unable to stop themselves. There was a crash, and shouts of pain. That was two more who were probably out of the race. A few bruises can dampen anyone's enthusiasm for a fight.

Meanwhile, me, Sam and Cappo had climbed up the other wall, getting ourselves to high ground, and were sitting on top of it, rummaging through our kit bag. In seconds, we had between us three packs of eggs. We'd nicked them from my fridge at home; they were in those cardboard padded cartons, and one look at them revealed that they'd almost all remained uncracked. One of Cappo's was oozing cold yolk, but we still had seventeen or so good eggs that we could use to pelt the poor saps with as they mired themselves in the trash of the alleyway. I was fairly slavering in anticipation.

"This one's okay!" someone shouted. Presumably, he'd found the safe plank that we had set up to get over the wall. They used it. I could hardly believe the electric excitement as the dark figures came over the wall, howling at us. There wasn't any rush like it.

"There they are!" the lead figure screamed, his voice embarrassingly high, as if he couldn't believe that we were cheeky enough to sit on that wall and *wait* for them to come. Obviously, the thought that we were laying a trap didn't cross his mind. But I kind of expected that from these guys.

We sat there, shouting abuse at them as they tried to make it up the alley towards us. The first one, an anonymous lad with shaved hair and an earring, got about three paces before the rubble under his feet suddenly shifted violently and he pitched over, smacking his forearms against the stones. The others, heedless of his misfortune, pounded on in there. I recognized Stew as one of the front-runners. With long strides, they tried one-by-one to run over the rubble towards us; and one-by-one, they all fell, bashing ankles, banging shins and bruising toes.

I could see Stew there, and Gary Donley. I watched Stew coming towards us, his eyes fixed on me in rage. I watched as the piece of rock that he put his front foot on suddenly turned, and I watched as his leg slipped away from him and he crashed into the back of one of his already fallen comrades.

We didn't wait for Gary Donley to tumble; we decided to help him along.

"Fire!" I shouted, and we opened up with the eggs, pelting them full-whack at the guys below us. It was like something out of the Keystone Kops, or one of those dodgy BBC children's dramas. I mean, there they were, flailing about like idiots on the floor, while we lobbed eggs at them and laughed as they exploded all over our pursuers, sliming them with yolk and albumen. They were apoplectic with fury, and their anger only made them more violent in their attempts to get us, and that only meant they fell over more, which made them madder, and so on. Honestly, we couldn't have done better if we had rolled marbles under their feet or something. That would have been less corny, I reckon.

Sam hit Gary Donley square in the face with an egg. "That one was personal," he jeered. I almost cried with laughter as Gary went toppling over backwards, crashing painfully to the ground. Sam leaned back, satisfied with his revenge. But our fun was suddenly spoiled by a chunk of brick that went whipping past my head, missing me by a few inches. My laughing stopped, and it took me a second to realize what had happened. Then it dawned on me, as I saw Stew grab another hunk of stone. This was another slight flaw in our plan. We hadn't thought that they might chuck the rubble at *us*!

We didn't need to communicate. All three of us hoisted ourselves over the wall and dropped down the other side, retreating under the hail of rocks as the other guys caught on to Stew's plan. The amusement had suddenly drained out of me. It wasn't like what we'd been doing to them; I mean, we'd been aiming to humiliate them and bruise them a bit, but a rock thrown like that could kill! I had forgotten what kind of guys we were dealing with. I couldn't help thinking that, if Danny was here, he'd have thought of that.

Where the hell was he, anyway?

There was one more alley between us and the main road. It was just about clear, running between the empty husks of an old school – which had a gaping hole in the wall where the service door used to be – and some kind of factory. It ended in a rusty gate which had been chained shut long ago. The last stretch to freedom. The theory was that the others would soon give up, banged and bruised as they were, and wouldn't bother following us out to the road and beyond. However, we had been a little overconfident, I reckon, because we were just starting to clamber over the gate when Stew dropped into the alley.

How he did it, I'll never know. I suppose that maybe he was mad enough to climb over the backs of his fallen friends to get to me. He certainly looked like he was almost insane with fury. I don't know why we didn't hang around and take him out – I mean, there were three of us – but the expression of unreasoning, animal hatred on his face made us realize that maybe this whole thing was a little more serious than we had thought.

Sam was already over the gate. It was an easy climb, with wide gaps in the wrought-iron frame which you could easily fit your foot through. Cappo was already half up it when Stew appeared, and he was almost over it when he slipped.

I should have known that it was going to happen. I mean, I knew at the time that it wasn't a good idea waking up Cappo to come along. He wasn't in much of a state for adventures, what with all that stuff about his parents' divorce, and all the drink inside him. It was a testament to how good a friend he was that he had come at all, and we had been oh-so-lucky that he hadn't wrongfooted it before now. It had to happen. He was drunk, and he slipped, and he fell.

Thankfully, I was there to catch him.

The next few seconds passed in a frantic blur. I

almost threw him up over the gate, not even giving him time to get his feet back under him, putting all my weight into giving him the boost he needed. Somehow, his foot connected with a foothold, and his hands gripped on to something solid. He practically fell over the top of the gate, completely disorientated and off-balance. But Cappo's pretty light, 'cause he's so thin. It was a hectic moment, and he could easily have fallen badly and broken something, but he didn't. Sam caught him heavily by the shoulders, Cappo's legs trailing down afterwards, and he was safely over.

I, on the other hand, was not.

Chapter Thirteen

There are moments in your life when you have to make decisions, and you just don't have time to think about them. And every way, you seem to lose. At that point, the passing of seconds slows obligingly to a crawl, so you can squeeze every last ounce of terror out of that moment of choice, knowing full well that the wrong move could result in things turning pretty bad for you.

It's the feeling you get when you're running towards the stream bank that your friends have just jumped over, knowing that you've got your stride all wrong, knowing that you'll never make that leap. You're going too fast to stop. Do you bail out and eat dirt, or do you make the jump and land in the water? Not much good either way, right? And your friends on the other side are totally unaware that, for you, almost a minute has passed for every second of their time.

That was what it was like for me. Did I try and make the jump over the gate to safety, and run the risk of Stew catching me before I got over it, or did I peg it through the old, crumbling doorway into the derelict school? One way, it was do or die. The other, it meant that I would be one-on-one with Stew (who was now firmly in INSANE mode) and the pursuit would still be on.

In the end, I didn't really have a choice. My instincts kind of decided for me. My senses were screaming at me, telling me (even though I couldn't see him) that Stew was *too* close, that he was going to catch me if I didn't move *now*!

I ducked left. I caught a last impression of the horrified faces of Sam and Cappo, neatly divided by the metal bars of the gate, and then I was outta there.

It all degenerated into a blur. Suddenly, I was inside the school, in a maze of darkness. Vague rectangles of light blue – doorways – flashed by as I stumbled through the rooms. The floor was mercifully clear, but I still had some narrow escapes as I ran headlong into the heart of the school. I could hear Stew behind me, his feet clumping heavily in pursuit; never close enough so that I could see him, but always there. I did doublebacks, switches, trying to get him off my tail, but I couldn't shake him.

Should I stand and fight it out with him? No. Remember what I said before about school fights and street fights? Well, Stew was absolutely nuts at the moment, and I didn't fancy losing a fight to him in the state he was in. He'd probably give me the beating of my life. I stopped short, almost running into a wall, as the corridor suddenly transformed into a stairwell, leading upwards. Damn! I didn't want to go up! That would really cut down my chances of getting out of this place.

"When I find you, you're *dead*!" Stew screamed,

his voice sounding terrifyingly close. I didn't hang around any more. It was up the stairs or nothing.

I came out in a long corridor, empty doorways running along either side of it. I presumed that they led into what used to be classrooms. It didn't matter; nothing was recognizable in this place any more. Everything worth salvaging had been salvaged. The rest of the place was all burned out. No furniture remained; no desks, no chairs, no cupboards. It had probably been long since stripped for the numerous bonfires staged in the Zone over the last few years. There was nowhere to hide in there.

Down the corridor I went, my shoes thudding on the floor, and I thought I could hear the sound of Stew pounding up the stairs behind me. I almost didn't dare to look, but there was something magnetic about my pursuer, drawing my eyes over my shoulder.

He was there, sprinting down the long corridor. He was gaining.

I poured on a fresh burst of speed, but I was rapidly running out of corridor. A blank wall of flaking concrete, its decay highlighted in the blue night-glow, rushed forward to meet me. I cursed whoever had built this place for giving it such a straightforward layout.

No. I *refused* to be trapped in this corridor.

Then I saw it: a small, recessed alcove with a beckoning doorway, right at the end of the corridor. The door, like all the others, had long since disappeared. I rushed inside, grateful for any chance to escape ... and found myself staring at another stairwell. Going up.

Again, no choice. No time to think. I raced up it, realizing that it must be some kind of roof access for the caretaker. Undoubtedly, in years gone by, it would have been kept locked to prevent pupils from coming up here; but time and vandals had long since dealt with that. At the top, however, there was a metal door.

I almost ran into it, only stopping myself by thrusting my hands out in front of me to take the force of my momentum. I had got so used to the absence of doors in this place that this one really surprised me. However, it took me only a second for my surprise to turn to concern. This door was blocking my only way out!

I grabbed the handle and pulled. No good. It wasn't budging. I tried again, this time throwing all my weight into the effort. Again, it didn't budge. At the bottom of the stairs, I heard the rapidly approaching clump of Stew's feet. I couldn't fight him on the stairwell! Frantically, I tugged the door again, pleading with the steel. It ignored me and stayed shut.

Stew appeared at the bottom of the stairs, his dark outline running into view. He saw me and stopped. I was trapped and he knew it. Both of us were panting heavily, our rasping breaths the only sounds until he spoke.

"You are *so* dead," he growled.

Hang on. This was a roof-access door, right? Why would it swing inward when there were stairs here? It opens *outwards*! I shouldn't be pulling, I should be pushing!

I slammed my shoulder to the door. It burst open, and I flew through it into the night air, my feet already working to give me a lead over Stew. He cried out in surprise, starting up the stairs after me. The door rebounded from the force of my blow, slamming shut in his face; but a second later, he had kicked it open again, steaming after me like a maddened bull.

The roof of the school was broad and flat, with only a few skylights and air vents poking up to ruin the uniformity. It looked like an alien landscape in the shadows of night, strange structures looming out of nowhere, bizarre and unsettling. The Zone stretched away all around, a multitude of dead buildings, all silently watching me, goblin-faces in black, glowering windows.

I ran to the edge and looked over, leaning against the safety barrier. The barrier ran all the way around the rooftop, a thick stone shelf that was roughly knee-high. I found myself looking down upon the narrow alley that I had first escaped from, the one with the gate where I had got separated from Cappo and Sam. The rooftop of the nearby factory leaned tantalizingly close, across the gulf of the alleyway. I looked back. Stew was cutting across the roof towards me, taking the most direct route. I had nowhere to run to.

I looked back across the alley. Could I make the jump? My common sense was screaming at me: *No! No!* But I was still a bit drunk, and my judgement wasn't A-1, and I reckoned that I could do it. The ultimate movie escape. No way would Stew have the nerve to follow me. I reckoned I would have jumped, too, and probably killed myself, if Danny hadn't shouted to me then.

"Jay! Get over here!"

I couldn't believe it. My head snapped around to pinpoint the sound of his voice, and there he was, on the other roof, across the alley, a few metres along from where I was standing. Danny! The point man was back! Questions jostled for position in my mind – where had he been? how had he found me? – but I knew that there wasn't time to answer them now. I ran over to him, conscious all the time of the approaching footsteps of Stew. I could imagine my pursuer, his arms swinging, legs pumping madly, bearing down on me. This time I didn't dare look.

Bridging the gap between the buildings was a long, fat, industrial-sized plank of wood. Danny was holding one end.

We didn't need to talk. I knew what he wanted me to do. I looked at him, disbelieving, as if to say: *you expect me to cross* that? What he was thinking, I couldn't say. But it was Stew or the bridge.

Sod it.

Stew was almost upon me, I could feel it. Without thinking about anything, without knowing if the plank could bear my weight, without questioning if Danny could hold it straight or not, I took one step back, jumped on to the safety barrier and *ran* on to the plank. There was no thought. There was only trust. Danny literally held my life in his hands.

For three of the longest seconds of my existence, I was running over a plank of wood only two feet wide, and a quarter-foot thick, suspended over a drop of two storeys on to a hard, unforgiving, concrete floor. I saw Danny grit his teeth, stabilizing the plank with all the force he could muster.

Touchdown.

My feet hit the factory rooftop, and there was a sudden rush of the most awesome euphoria I had ever felt in my life. At the same moment, I heard the bone-chilling sound of sliding wood as Danny let go of the end of the plank, and it pitched over and toppled into the alley below.

For a few sickening seconds, there was silence as it fell. I could so easily imagine myself falling that distance. Then it hit the floor with an almighty clatter, and I had collapsed to my knees on the rooftop, a big, stupid grin on my face.

"You *bastard*!" Stew howled, and then Danny was helping me to my feet, and I saw my enemy on the other side of the gap, bellowing with rage, kicking the low safety barrier in frustration.

"See you next time, *loser*," I replied, unable to resist that one last comeback. Like all the best action movies, the hero had to have the last word. Otherwise, it just wasn't right.

I turned my back on him, and we were out of there, Danny taking point again, zooming into the bowels of the factory, on our way to safety. Stew would never catch us now. Me and my Zone Runners had done it.

Mission accomplished.

Chapter Fourteen

We were practically floating on the trip back across the fields to my house. Behind us, I could almost imagine the Zone brooding sullenly at our departure. We had beaten Stew and his gang, and we had survived the Zone unscathed. What a team!

Cappo and Sam were mock-boxing with each other, still full of pent-up energy. Me and Danny were walking a little more sedately, the grass rustling underneath our feet, a light breeze beginning to stir our hair. It must have been two or three o'clock in the morning by now.

Looking up at the stars, I realized that it was over. I'd done it, I reckoned. The events of the party had created a rift between us, but uniting against Stew had reminded us all how important our friends were to us. And I thought to myself: if we can go through the kind of trials we did tonight and still be friends at the end of it all, then what on earth am I worried about? We're gonna be friends for ever.

"Some night, huh?" said Danny, grinning at me.

"It's been ... *interesting*," I said, understating massively. Danny laughed.

"Yeah, you could say that. You know, I'm never gonna forget that moment when you ran across that plank, Jay. Better than *this*" – he pulled Ian Hun-tingdon's keyring out of his pocket – "better than anything. I don't think I've ever seen anything so cool in my life."

"I don't think I've ever done anything so *stupid* in my life," I replied, but I was looking at the keyring in his hand and thinking what a huge compliment he had just paid me.

"You got away with it, right? So stop griping. Anyway, we showed Stew what for. Or should I say, you guys did."

"Which reminds me," I said. "Where did you get off to after you got chased out of the factory?"

Danny looked down at his hands, scratching one thumbnail against the other in an attempt to remove some welded-on muck. "I got sidetracked. First, I didn't know if those guys were gonna follow me out or not, so I had to put some distance between me and them. Then I ran into another bunch of guys – prob-ably the friends of those two in the factory – and I had to split before they saw me. After that ... well, I got lost, to be honest with you."

"So how did you find me afterwards?"

"Easy enough. I did what we suggested in the first place: I got to some high ground, and looked for bonfires. I ended up finding my way back to the Square, and from there I knew how to get to the car park that we'd been talking about. I got there just as you were starting the fireworks. Awesome job, by the way."

"Couldn't have done it without your patented cap-bangers," I replied modestly.

"Well, I couldn't follow you, 'cause all Stew's mates were after you. Besides, I guessed that you'd booby-trapped that whole stretch of alleys; and judging by the howls, I was right. That was always our trademark, wasn't it? The stylish escape." He prodded me playfully. "So I took the long way round. I was gonna meet you on the main road, but on the way I heard Stew screaming at you, and I guessed you were in trouble. So I dodged into the building that I thought the sound came from, but I picked the wrong one. That's how I ended up on the factory roof, while you were in the school."

"Well, Danny," I said, putting my arm round his shoulders, "you are just a miracle."

"I try," he shrugged coyly. Then his face went a little serious. "Listen, Jay. I noticed on the way into the Zone that there was a bit of tension going on between you and Sam."

"Yeah," I said. Danny had reminded me about Sam and Jo. While we were in the Zone, I had barely thought about her in all the excitement; but now it was over, I found it was still a problem to be faced. And I needed to face it.

"Hey, Sam," I called. He stopped trying to jab at Cappo and looked at me. "Can I talk to you for a minute?"

"Sure," he said, shrugging.

From over my shoulder, Danny said: "If you're looking for someone to beat your ass, Cappo, I'm your man."

"Yeah?" Cappo cried back. "In your dreams, laughing boy!"

With that, they pounced on each other and started wrestling in the grass.

Me and Sam walked on a little way, until the sounds of combat had receded a little. "So what's on your mind?" said Sam. I looked at him. Again, I was struck by how enviably handsome he was, even in the gloom. Maybe Jo did deserve better than me. She was certainly pretty enough. Maybe she and Sam would be better for each other.

I sighed, a bit sad. "I just wanted to say, you know, about you and Jo. It's cool with me, I guess. You know how I get over girls sometimes."

"Yeah, I know. It's alright," said Sam, a little flat. He wasn't much good at expressing emotions to other guys. "It might not have been such a good idea to fly off the handle at Jo, though. She's probably not as forgiving as me."

"I suppose not," I admitted.

"Especially as we didn't do anything," Sam added.

I stopped in my tracks. Sam walked on a few paces before noticing that I wasn't walking with him any more, then turned round.

"What?" I said dumbly. I always say that when someone says something shocking to me. I wish my mental reactions were a tad faster.

Sam shrugged. "Well, we didn't," he said. He sounded almost apologetic. "I've got to admit, I thought about it. Maybe I even tried it on a little. But we didn't do anything."

"Why didn't you *tell* me?" I cried.

"I just did," Sam replied obtusely.

144

"I mean, *before.*"

He gazed at me levelly. "Would you have believed me? Besides, by the time I saw you, you had already accused Jo, and you weren't even speaking to me." His face took on a sort of piteous expression. "I mean, I'll be the first to admit that I've got a bit of a reputation, but do you really think that *any* girl is going to jump on me when we're left for two minutes alone together?" He looked at me wryly, before lapsing into a sinister East European accent. "I think you overestimate me, Mr Bond."

But I'd suddenly lost the urge to laugh. Oh, how could I have been so stupid? The more I thought about it, the more ridiculous it seemed. Sam was right; I *did* think that he had the ability to make women fall at his feet. And it was something that I'd always been jealous of. I don't think I'd ever realized just *how* jealous until now. If it had been anybody else that I saw coming out of that room with Jo, I would have given them the benefit of the doubt. But not Sam.

I realized then how badly I'd let myself down. I'd had no faith in either Jo or Sam. I'd automatically assumed the worst, and acted on it without even waiting for an explanation. Why didn't I *think*? But that's what girls do to me. They stop me thinking, and they mess up my priorities. I should have trusted my friend. And I should have trusted Jo.

"So what *were* you doing in the bedroom?" I asked Sam.

Sam glanced at me sympathetically. "You don't wanna know."

"I do," I insisted. "Tell me."

He sighed. "She'd dragged me in there to talk to me about you. She wanted to know about you. She wanted to know if you fancied her, or if you were going for a one-night thing. Stuff like that."

I groaned. "I must be the dumbest person alive today," I lamented.

Sam scuffed his feet. "I'd say so. She was really up for it, Jay. She really liked you. And you've blown it."

That really fired me. He was right, of course; but I couldn't let it rest at that. She was the last part of the jigsaw. So far, I'd dragged myself back from the brink of despair tonight, turned defeat into victory, and transformed this party from a disaster into one of the best nights of my life. Only one thing remained: Jo. And I wasn't going to let her go that easily.

"Blown it, huh?" I said. "Not yet, I haven't."

And with that, I began to run across the fields, back towards my house, praying that it wasn't already too late.

I arrived, breathless, in my back garden. Pushing my way through the barrier of trees that had sheltered me and my troops during the High Noon face-off between my forces and Stew's, I stepped into sight of my house again. The security light was still on, flooding the rear façade with brightness. I could see, through the patio door, that people were still fooling around in the lounge. Most of the the bedroom lights were off.

But none of that held my attention. What I saw was

Jo, sitting in one of the white plastic chairs at one of the circular tables, with the parasol open (absurdly) as if to shade her from the minimal moonlight. Sitting with her was Pete. They were both talking animatedly. I heard Jo laugh, distance carrying her voice to me.

I was filled with relief, suddenly. For a time, I had been sure that Jo would have gone to sleep by now, and that I'd never get a chance to try and sort things out with her. She didn't know many people at this party, and with me (and Sam) gone, I thought that she'd have little to stay up for. But bless him: Pete Baker, my sci-fi-obsessed buddy had engaged her, and she obviously wasn't ready to quit yet. Besides, she was a clubber girl; she was used to staying up till six in the morning.

It may seem contradictory, but I'm not really a jealous guy. Honestly. That was why it was so out of character, the way I reacted to Sam. So when I saw Pete Baker with Jo, I didn't feel jealous of him at all. Besides, I'm not the most attractive guy around, but the day that Pete Baker pulls the girl I can't is the day that I become celibate. And hadn't I seen him with Kerry Macclesfield not so long ago? For Pete to get a girl twice in one night would break several major laws of universal physics.

I walked across the garden towards them, getting my breath back as I went. As I neared, I noticed the broken shards of glass that were scattered across the patio from my window. Well, the smashed window was tomorrow's problem. It was just my word against Gary's that he put the brick through it; and, after all, if I told my parents about him, I'd have to tell them about the party, and that was something that I didn't fancy much. Maybe I could blag it as an accident (after removing the brick, of course; you can't *accidentally* throw a brick through a window) or maybe I'd have to pay for it myself. Sod it; a small sacrifice for the good times I'd had tonight.

They were drinking their beers and chatting to each other, with a kind of laid-back ease that was certainly unusual in Pete. They didn't see me till the last minute, when I had almost reached them.

"Hi, Jay," Pete called suddenly, then glanced at Jo and flushed guiltily. She'd obviously told him what I'd done, and he feared that I'd beat him up or something for "muscling in on my girl". He needn't have worried, though. That was Stew's style, not mine.

Jo didn't say anything. She just sort of acknowledged me with a nod.

There was a spare chair around the table. I motioned to it. "Do you mind if I sit down?"

"It's your home," Jo said.

"I didn't ask that," I said, patiently. "I asked if you minded."

"I don't mind," she said, dismissive. Ouch, this was gonna be hard.

"Pete?" I asked.

"Course not," he said hastily.

I sat down. Pete picked up a can that was lying by his chair – it was still attached to those little plastic loops you get around six-packs – and gave it to me.

"You look like you need it," he said. "I don't want any more, anyway."

"Thanks," I said, very genuine. Right now, that beer seemed like the most heavenly thing in the world. I pulled off the plastic loops, chucked them aside, popped it and drank.

"I'm gonna go, anyway," said Pete. "I'd better go find Kerry."

"Don't go because of me," I said, though this was more for Jo's benefit than anything else. Obviously, I wanted him to leave so I could talk to her; but I didn't want it to *look* like I wanted him to leave.

"Nah, I'd better," he insisted. Good old Pete; he knew what he was doing. "I'll see you both."

"Yeah, see you," said Jo, touching his arm as he went past. "Do you wanna borrow that video sometime?"

"Sure. I'll talk to you in the morning, okay?" said Pete, retreating clumsily.

"Okay."

Then he was gone. There was silence. Me and Jo looked at each other across the table.

"Video?" I asked, making small talk.

"Me and Pete discovered that we were both into Anime cartoons. You know, Japanese animation? Manga and A. D. Vision and stuff." She indicated the stylized cutesy spaceman on her T-shirt. "We decided we were gonna trade some videos."

"Oh, right," I said.

There was silence again. I took a mental breath. This wasn't going to be easy. But I had to do it. I couldn't live with myself if I flaked out and let her go.

"There's some things I want to talk to you about, Jo."

Jo leaned back cynically. "Okay. Shoot."

I took a swig of beer, swallowed hard. "I want to tell you that I was wrong," I began. "I'm sorry for what I said to you before, about Sam. I know I didn't trust you – I didn't trust *either* of you – and I was stupid. I want you to know I'm sorry, that's all. I don't ... have any kind of excuse or anything. That's all I can say."

It didn't go as I expected. She didn't melt into my arms with a sigh of "Oh, Jay" and forgive me in an instant for being manly enough to admit my mistakes. Instead, she folded her arms across her chest and regarded me icily with those (*gorgeous*) oriental eyes. I swear, it never went like that in the movies. Sod it. I was lied to by my idols.

"That's all you've got to say?" she demanded.

"That's all I *can* say," I repeated. "I can make it up to you, but only if you let me."

"Oh? And how's that?"

I hadn't really expected that one. I hadn't thought that far ahead. "I don't know," I replied, after an agonizingly embarrassing pause.

"Good answer," she said, sarcastically. Then, before I could reply, she continued, "You aren't *that* special, you know. And it would take someone pretty damn special to make me forgive them after what you did. We'd barely been talking for a few hours and

150

already you were acting like you owned me! I'm not your *property*, you know?"

"No, no," I replied, floundering for the right thing to say. "It wasn't you ... it was ... it was only because it was Sam, that's all. I don't know if you know about his reputation with girls, but..."

"So is that how you see girls? Mindlessly leaping on the most attractive guy of the bunch if he just bats his lashes at them?"

Damn it, it was like she was going out of her way to be awkward! She was picking up on every little nuance of what I said and turning it against me.

"That wasn't what I said!" I protested.

"But it was what you were thinking!" she countered. I'd walked into that one. Boy, did she have me on the ropes.

"You don't know what I'm thinking," I shot back. "If you did, you wouldn't be making it so bloody hard for me to explain myself!" That was a counterstrike and a half.

"What's to explain?" she replied, not giving me a second's breathing space. "You called me a slag earlier. I think that's pretty—"

"Since when did I call you a slag?" I interrupted, incredulous.

"You thought I'd got off with Sam when I'd promised to stick around and wait for you to get back. I'd say that's pretty close."

"No, it's not. I never owned you. You can do what the hell you want!" I was getting ever-so-slightly angry now at the way she was steering this argument. Or was it frustration that I couldn't seem to win?

"Oh, you didn't own me? Well, you sure acted like you did!"

"What is your obsession with being *owned*, anyway? Did you get locked in a trunk as a kid or something?" Now I was getting silly. I just wanted to beat her now, I didn't care about anything else. I'd apologized to her, and she'd blown me out. Well, I'd done my bit. And if I wasn't able to make things up with her, the least I could do was go out on a winner.

But she didn't reply. For a moment she looked at me with an expression of stunned amazement, then she burst out laughing. I mean, *really* laughing, like how me and Sam and Cappo started laughing in the Zone; real rib-aching, throat-stripping laughter.

"That," she gasped, when she could snatch a breath, "was the stupidest put-down I've ever heard!"

The last few words dissolved into another screaming peal of mirth. And she was right. I could see the funny side. And I began to laugh, too.

When we had both finally stopped, I was feeling really good again. I swear, laughter is nature's antidote to all your problems. I'd been angry before, but now . . . now I was just happy. Whatever happened, I was happy.

"So," I said. "Am I gonna see you again?"

"You've got some cheek," she replied, "after what you did."

"Come on," I said. "It was a mistake. It wasn't High Treason."

She seemed to think. Then she got up, her chair screeching along the tiles. "I'm going to sleep," she said. Her face was neutral. "I'll probably be gone early in the morning."

"What about it, though?" I said. "Can I call you?"

"It's a free country," she replied, as she walked away towards the back door of the house.

"Okay then," I said, rephrasing. "If I do call you, will you answer?"

"Maybe," I heard her say. "Maybe not."

As she said those words, she was disappearing into the kitchen, and she had her back to me. She didn't think I could see her face, but I could see a little. And I saw the secret smile she allowed herself as she left, a private smile, one that she didn't expect me to see. And I knew then that she had just been making me suffer, that she had just wanted to see me squirm, and that she had really forgiven me from the moment I had told her I was sorry. That whole argument, her whole unreasonable attitude; it had all been for her own enjoyment. She'd just wanted to watch me sweat.

Girls. Who could figure them? I thought, as I sat alone on my back porch, a great big grin plastered over my face.

And then, looking up past the frilled rim of the parasol at the stars in the night sky, I suddenly remembered something that Jo had said only a few minutes ago. *"It would take someone pretty damn special to make me forgive them after what you did."*

Jo was gonna be my girlfriend.

Al*right.*

About the author

Chris Wooding was born in Leicester in 1977, and hasn't done a whole lot since. He's just finished a degree in English Literature at Sheffield University, and is living in Leicester at the moment because it's the best place he knows.

CRASHING was written when he was nineteen, during a summer holiday when he had nothing better to do.